*A
Harlequin
Romance*

OTHER
Harlequin Romances
by JANICE GRAY

Many of these titles are available at your local bookseller,
or through the Harlequin Reader Service.

For a free catalogue listing all available Harlequin Romances,
send your name and address to:

HARLEQUIN READER SERVICE,
M.P.O. Box 707, Niagara Falls, N.Y. 14302
Canadian address: Stratford, Ontario, Canada N5A 6W4

or use coupon at back of books.

LULLABY OF LEAVES

by

JANICE GRAY

HARLEQUIN BOOKS   TORONTO
WINNIPEG

Original hard cover edition published in 1969
by Mills & Boon Limited

SBN 373-01931-9

Harlequin edition published December 1975

Printed in Canada

1931

For Dodie
(Doris Acland)
with much love

CHAPTER ONE

'CAN you please take us to Brocade?'

Francesca Norton looked anxiously at the one and only taxi driver she had noticed anywhere in the vicinity of the little railway station, wondering uneasily if the name 'Brocade' was sufficient identification, even if it was supposed to be one of England's stately homes.

She felt her heart sink as the man hesitated perceptibly, but it transpired that his hesitancy was due not so much to unfamiliarity with the area as to a strong suspicion that Fran had made a mistake.

'You did say Brocade, ma'am? You're sure that's where you want to go?'

The incredulous note in his voice made Fran tilt her chin. 'Certainly I'm sure. Can you take us?'

The taxi driver still hesitated. 'I've only got a mini-cab. There's rather a lot of you, ain't there?'

He scanned the little group dubiously. Besides Fran, there were five young children, all unprepossessingly crumpled, tousled and travel-stained, and a pile of somewhat battered suitcases which had certainly seen better days. No, it seemed hardly feasible that they wanted Brocade, the splendid old Tudor mansion which in bygone years had entertained Royalty beneath its ancient roof!

'Oh, please!' Fran's voice was imploring. 'We've been travelling for *hours*—and the children are so tired! They don't take up an awful lot of room, I promise you. We can all sit on each other's laps.'

'I'm firsty. Want a drink!' The youngest child, a fair-haired mite with huge blue eyes, spoke fretfully. Looking at her, Fran realised with dismay that she was

7

about to cry. She did this but rarely, being a singularly phlegmatic small mortal on the whole, but her tears, once started, were apt to go on for ever and were at all costs to be avoided.

Six pleading pairs of eyes were fixed on the taxi driver's face. A family man, he surrendered, albeit reluctantly.

'All right! Give me your luggage!'

With commendable efficiency he marshalled the tired children into his tiny vehicle and somehow or other managed to stow away the conglomeration of bags and suitcases.

'All set, missus?'

Missus...? For a moment Fran's astonishment was reflected in her face, then a rueful smile touched her lips. Of course she was wearing gloves ... he wouldn't have had a chance to notice her ringless hands. Did he by any chance imagine that she was the mother of this entire brood? No wonder he'd given her such a pitying look!

She settled herself back in her seat and wondered half-heartedly if there was anything they could do to tidy themselves up before they reached Brocade. At the moment they must look a thoroughly disreputable bunch and she could only hope that the housekeeper there wouldn't be taken too much aback! Anyway, whatever her reaction it couldn't be helped. It had been impossible to keep the children clean and tidy on that filthy train!

'Will you be stayin' at Brocade long?' It was evident that the taxi driver's curiosity had been aroused.

It was not Fran who answered him, however, but the children.

'Until our house is ready for us again. It got burned down.' That, of course, was Danny.

'It didn't.' That was his younger sister, Beanie, firmly correcting him. 'It just got burned a little bit.'

8

'The firemen came.' Another eager voice chimed in. 'And two fire engines! They squirted water *everywhere*!'

Thank goodness, thought Fran as she listened to the ingenuous confidences, that they now looked back upon that dreadful night as something in the nature of an adventure. She'd never be able to do that, not as long as she lived. Even now, remembering the roar of the greedy flames and the clouds of black, stifling smoke as she'd hustled the children to safety, she felt sick in the pit of her stomach. The fire hadn't been her fault ... she'd told Peter so many times that he must never smoke in bed ... but just the same she felt responsible. A housemother employed by the Greater London Council, for the last eighteen months she'd been in charge of what was known as a 'small family' home and looked after ten children whose ages ranged from four to sixteen. Normally she had an assistant housemother to help her, a pretty, dark-haired Irish girl, but for the last fortnight Patsy had been in hospital and on the night of the fire she'd been alone in the house with the children.

It might have been so much worse! The only casualty had been Peter, who had broken a leg when jumping in panic out of his bedroom window. And the house itself hadn't been too badly damaged, though repairs and renovations would take several weeks. It had seemed, though, that in the meantime the children would have to be split up and sent to other Homes, something which everyone wanted to avoid but which seemed inescapable. Then Margot Eliot had taken a hand. One of the youngest and liveliest members of the Child Care Committee, she had promptly issued an invitation to Fran and the children to spend a few weeks at Brocade, in the heart of the Cotswolds. It belonged, she had explained to Miss Challoner, the Children's Officer, to her cousin, but he was abroad and except for the housekeeper the house was unoccupied.

'It's been empty for months, apparently, ever since the last owner, Mrs. Eliot's uncle, died,' Miss Challoner had told Fran. 'The new owner hasn't been home yet to claim his inheritance and goodness knows when he will come. In the meantime, as Mrs. Eliot says, there's a perfectly good house going to waste and you and the children badly in need of a roof over your heads. What could be more providential?'

Nothing could, and so here they were on their way to Brocade. Not all the children: Peter was still in hospital and his younger sister, Pauline, had elected to stay behind in order to be near him. Three others, 'short-term' cases only, had been fitted into existing Homes. But Fran felt that she still had the nucleus of her family: eight-and-a-half-year-old Robin, seven-year-old Mark, six-year-old Danny, five-year-old Beanie and three-year-old Sue.

She became aware that the taxi driver was looking at her curiously, and flushed. She did not realise that in her crisp cotton dress, with her pale gold hair wind-tossed, she looked scarcely old enough to be the mother of Sue, let alone the others. The taxi driver scented a mystery and for the rest of the journey plied her with questions. She struggled to answer with civility, but she had her work cut out, for she also had Sue on her lap, was trying to persuade Beanie that she didn't really feel car-sick and prevent Mark and Danny, who both wanted to sit next to a window, from coming to blows. She could not help breathing a sigh of relief when at last, after careering through miles of delightfully unspoilt countryside, the taxi driver triumphantly announced that they were nearing journey's end.

They were chugging, at that moment, along a narrow winding lane running up a steep hill. At the very crest of the hill stood a long, low house, built of honey-coloured stone, with an irregular roof and shining windows of all shapes and sizes, most of them mullioned and with small diamond panes of wavy glass.

Fran knew without being told that this was Brocade. It was one of the loveliest old houses she had ever seen, and its setting was perfect. As they swept up the drive she caught a glimpse of smooth velvety lawns starred by many-hued clumps of flowers and bordered by mighty oaks. The effect of the bright colours against the delicate green of the carefully tended grass made her catch her breath, then the car drew up by a stone balustrade which separated the garden from a long terrace which ran the whole length of the house. There was a loud blast on the horn, the great oak front door opened and a woman, obviously Mrs. Henderson, came out. Small, plump and grey-haired, she ran down the two sets of steps which led to the lawn, her white apron billowing before her, and greeted Fran with a warmth which took her completely by surprise.

'Here you are at last! And the children—oh, the poor lambs! They look tired to death!' She turned to the taxi driver. 'You'll see to the luggage, won't you? Give me the little girl, miss, I'll carry her in.'

Sue, thumb in mouth, was nearly asleep. Thankfully Fran relinquished her to the waiting arms and turned to pay the driver and to help the other children to scramble out of the car. Her fears of a stiff, starchy housekeeper who would bitterly resent their intrusion were fast disappearing into limbo. There was nothing remotely unwelcoming about Mrs. Henderson—in fact, her rosy face was wreathed in smiles and her manner could not have been warmer had they been distinguished guests.

She led them up the shallow steps and into a cool, spacious hall which was bathed in a mellow glow as the early evening sunshine poured in through the stained-glass window, throwing coloured lights on to the polished floor. The walls were panelled in dark oak, there were bowls of golden roses on the window-sills and there was a sheen on the beautiful antique furniture which bespoke hours of loving care.

Fran suddenly found herself going hot with em-barrassment as mentally she contrasted their own dis-hevelled state with the gleaming perfection of their surroundings. She looked at the housekeeper and found that there was an understanding twinkle in the shrewd black eyes.

'Baths first, I think,' she said judicially. 'Supper afterwards. You see to the little boys and I'll look after the girls. Two bathrooms. Plenty of hot water.'

'But, Mrs. Henderson, you can't——'

'Many hands make light work,' Mrs. Henderson said firmly.

Fran gave in. Instinctively she recognised the house-keeper as one of those women born to care for chil-dren, and Sue and Beanie seemed to recognise that fact too. Willingly they surrendered themselves into hands whose skill they knew they could trust.

It was like a miracle. In an amazingly short space of time the children were undressed, bathed, fed and in bed, pink, shining, replete and comforted. Danny, Robin and Mark were in one big, airy bedroom, Sue and Beanie were in another, slightly smaller, room and Fran had a large room to herself, overlooking the velvet lawns.

'We must have made you so much work——' Fran still felt, half guiltily, that apologies were called for, but Mrs. Henderson pooh-poohed her immediately.

'Gracious me, I don't mind the work! 'Tis glad I am to have somebody to keep me company, and that's the truth! This house feels three times as big as it really is when it's empty, and there's not a soul has stayed here since Sir Antony died last year. A crying shame, it is.' She looked sharply at Fran, who was almost swaying on her feet from sheer weariness. 'Now what about a nice bath for you, miss, while I'm getting your supper?'

Fran made one last effort. 'Look, Mrs. Henderson, I honestly don't expect to be waited on. It's terribly kind of you, but——'

'No buts!' the housekeeper said firmly. 'We'll get on better, miss, if you let me do things my way. Just run yourself a nice hot bath. Afterwards—well, we'll have to talk things over, won't we? But believe me, I'm only too glad to have someone to look after, it's a nice change after so many months on my own!'

Fran surrendered with a laugh. Mrs. Henderson so obviously meant what she said.

'She's nice, isn't she?' Beanie said drowsily as Fran went in to tuck her up. 'I'm glad we're here.'

'So am I,' Fran assured her, dropping a kiss on the smooth brown head. Sue was already fast asleep, and as usual Fran removed her thumb from her mouth. For a moment the small chubby hand lay where Fran had placed it, then it moved upwards and the thumb popped back into the rosy mouth.

'Hopeless!' said Fran, laughing, and went into the boys' room. Danny, tousle-haired and bright-eyed, sat up in bed immediately he saw her.

'Can we go exploring when we wake up tomorrow?'

'After breakfast. Ssssh!' as Danny gave a whoop of joy. 'You'll wake the others!'

'I'm not asleep.' Mark spoke reproachfully. 'You haven't told us a story tonight.'

'Oh, Mark!' Fran laughed. 'I thought you'd be too tired to want one! What about two tomorrow night instead? Look, Robin really *is* asleep,' and she tucked the bedclothes round the small thin body. Not that it was really necessary—Robin always slept tidily, his face snuggled into the pillow. He was a tadpole of a boy with shy brown fawn's eyes and thin cheeks, one of which had been badly scarred with a red-hot poker when he was little more than a baby. A prison

13

sentence, in Robin's father's case, had been richly deserved.

'All right.' For once Mark, who always liked to get his own way, did not argue. He relaxed with what was almost undoubtedly a sigh of pure content and his dark lashes drooped. Mark was the 'handsome' one of Fran's family, with his dark curly hair, regular features and exquisitely cut lips, curved now into a contented smile. They were going to be happy here, Fran thought gladly as she made her way to the bathroom. This old house had the most marvellous atmosphere: it seemed to welcome, enfold and protect.

She bathed quickly and changed her dress before making her way down to the kitchen. Mrs. Henderson looked up from bending over the stove.

'My, you've been quick!' she said approvingly. 'Do you mind having supper in here? I always do: it's nice and cosy, to my way of thinking.'

'I quite agree with you.' Fran looked appreciatively around her, at the red tiled floor, the shining copper pots and pans, the gay china on the dresser and the sunshine yellow curtains at the big window. 'It's a lovely kitchen. But the whole house is marvellous, isn't it?'

'I'll show you round after supper.' Mrs. Henderson bustled forward with a bowl of soup. 'Of course, most of the rooms are shut up and all the furniture covered with dust sheets.' Her voice was tinged with regret. 'It's been like that for years. There was only Sir Antony and he wasn't much of a one for visitors.'

'Have you ever seen Mrs. Eliot, or the new owner?' Fran began to drink the hot soup gratefully.

'Mrs. Eliot's been here once or twice since the funeral. A nice lady, she is. I've never seen Mr. Richard—him what owns the house now, that is. He's been in South Africa for years: I sometimes wonder whether he ever will come home.' She sighed. 'I wish he would! That's just what this house needs—a nice young couple and a family of children to liven things up a bit!'

'He's married, then?'

Mrs. Henderson shook her head. 'Not as far as I know, but then there's precious little I *do* know about him. All my dealings are with Mrs. Eliot. It's a pity Sir Antony didn't leave the house to *her*. She would never let it go to rack and ruin!'

'Oh, hardly that!' Fran protested, laughing. 'I was thinking how well-kept everything looked.'

The housekeeper flushed with pleasure. 'That's nice of you, miss. I must own I take a pride in keeping things nice, as far as I can, but there's a lot more needs doing. Same with the garden. Sam does wonders, but he isn't as young as he used to be and he's only got a lad from the village to help him.' She hesitated. 'You'll not let the children run wild in the garden, miss? Sam, he wouldn't like it. But there's the shrubbery, and the woods, and the home meadow...'

'I'll try to make sure they don't upset him,' Fran promised. 'But——' She hesitated in her turn.

'Bit of a handful sometimes, are they?' Mrs. Henderson asked sympathetically. 'Well, you don't have to tell me that there's not a child born who doesn't get into mischief once in a way. I've had five sons meself, so I should know.'

Fran reflected wryly that it was unlikely that Mrs. Henderson *did* know. None of her family would ever have had to cope with the burdens and stresses experienced from birth by the average child 'in care'. It was hardly surprising that such children often presented many difficulties in their behaviour, though care, control, love and understanding usually worked wonders. She only hoped that there wouldn't be any desperate problems while they were at Brocade. There shouldn't be—as far as Mick, Beanie, Danny, Robin and Sue were concerned, really bizarre behaviour was a thing of the past.

The housekeeper was looking at her curiously. 'What is it they call you? A housemother?'

'That's my official title. The younger children started off by calling me Auntie, but then they copied the older ones and I became "Fran" to them all.'

'Seems a funny sort of a job for a girl like you, if you don't mind me saying so, miss.'

Fran laughed. 'I don't see why?'

'Well ... you're so pretty, aren't you?' Mrs. Henderson said bluntly. 'I'd have thought you'd have been married by now, with children of your own.'

Fran winced. The housekeeper meant no harm, but she'd touched a raw nerve. She looked down at her smooth brown hands. There was nothing now to show that she'd ever worn a sapphire ring on the third finger of her left hand. The ring that Bryan had put there the night he'd asked her to be his wife. They'd planned to get married at Christmas, but Bryan had met someone he liked better and a month before the wedding he'd written asking her to release him from their engagement. Not that it should matter now, after all these months. The flame of her love for Bryan had burnt out, and only the scar remained.

She said, as naturally as she could, 'Oh, I don't know. A ready-made family has advantages, don't you think?'

'I suppose so,' Mrs. Henderson said doubtfully. 'But it isn't much of a life for a young girl, is it? Wouldn't you have liked to do something more exciting ... something that didn't tie you down so much?'

Fran shook her head and laughed. 'I'm happy as I am, and what I'm doing is tremendously rewarding. Yes, really!' as Mrs. Henderson still looked dubious. 'I've always loved children, and those upstairs are really rather a jolly little bunch.'

'Are they all orphans?'

'Heavens, no!' Fran propped her chin in her hands. 'They're in care simply because there isn't anyone else

to look after them. Danny and Beanie, for instance—
their father was killed in a car crash and their mother
was terribly injured. She's still in hospital: she's been
in a coma for months.'

'Poor little souls!' Mrs. Henderson spoke warmly.
'Aren't there any relatives?'

'Plenty, but none willing to take the children. They
were being shunted about from pillar to post until we
took over.' Fran's voice was grim. She paused, then
added, 'Even so, they're luckier than some. They've
had such a rotten deal, most of the kids in our homes.'
She sighed. 'Take Peter and Pauline, for instance ...
the ones we've left behind in London. They've got
different fathers and their mother is a hopeless
alcoholic. She keeps promising she'll turn over a new
leaf and look after her family, but it's no good, she's
tried it once or twice and it's never worked out. Mark
... his mother deserted him two years ago, heaven
knows where she is now, and Father can't, or won't,
cope with the child. Robin was dreadfully ill-treated
by his parents—in fact, the father was sent to prison
for cruelty. Sue is the illegitimate daughter of a girl
who is mentally ill.'

Mrs. Henderson was silent for a moment. There was
a new respect in her eyes when she next spoke. 'I can
see what you mean when you say it's rewarding. But it
can't be an easy job.'

Fran laughed. 'Bringing up a family never is, is it?
Tell me about your sons, Mrs. Henderson. Are any of
them married, and have you got any grandchildren
yet?'

The housekeeper's face lit up and rather to Fran's
relief the recounting of her life history occupied the
rest of the meal.

CHAPTER TWO

AFTER supper, as she had promised, the housekeeper took Fran on a conducted tour of the big house.

'This is the library,' she said, coming at last to a panelled door at the left of the big curved staircase and opening it to show Fran a book-lined room. 'Sir Antony spent most of his time in here, he liked his books. Thousands of them, aren't there? Some of them are worth a mint of money, I believe, though who would give more than a few pence for one of those dusty old things I *don't* know, and that's a fact!' She gave a sound which was suspiciously like a snort.

Books ... Bryan. He had been something of an authority on rare and valuable volumes. How many hours had they spent in dingy second-hand bookshops, searching for the first editions which were his passion? Unbidden, unwanted, the intrusive memories came crowding back into her mind, and it was only with an effort that she jerked her thoughts back to the present.

She did not need to be told that the library had not been used since Sir Antony's death. It could, she thought, be an extremely pleasant room, but as of now it seemed cold and cheerless.

Above the beautiful Adam mantelpiece a portrait glowed against the dark panelling—a portrait of a stern-faced man with hard grey eyes, a strong chin, firmly-closed lips and the unmistakable air of an autocrat. Fran turned to Mrs. Henderson to ask the inevitable question.

'Is that—Sir Antony?'

'Yes. It was painted a good many years ago, of course. He was eighty when he died.'

'He never married?' There was no softness, no hint

18

of potential tenderness, in that bleak, forbidding face.

'No. He didn't have much time for women. I suppose that's why he didn't leave the house to Mrs. Eliot, though to my mind she deserved it far more than someone who never bothered about him once, not even when he was dying!'

There was an acid note in the housekeeper's voice as she closed the door on the library and they continued their tour. Despite her initial eagerness, Fran found it a strangely depressing experience. It seemed to her that the closed and shuttered rooms cried out to be opened up to life again, and she thought how unfair it was that such a beautiful old house should be kept waiting. Houses were like people, they needed to be loved.

'And this is *my* sitting room.' Mrs. Henderson showed Fran into a small, pleasant, flower-filled room, with deep comfortable armchairs, warm fitted carpet and cheerful curtains. 'I thought while you and the children were here you might like to make it yours. If it's too wet for them to go out they'll want somewhere to play, won't they?' She pointed to a large cupboard. 'When I was in the village this morning I bought a few games and books and jigsaws ... just to keep them going for a bit.'

Fran's eyes widened. 'Oh, *how* kind!' she exclaimed.

'Well, I want you to be happy here, you know.' Mrs. Henderson smiled at her. 'Poor little things, with no home of their own! Not but that I'm sure you do your best for them, miss!'—hastily—'but it isn't the same, is it?'

Fran thought of her own home, a large rectory in Norfolk which was nearly always filled with a comfortable conglomeration of people and pets; of her gentle, scholarly father and her sweet, vague, artistic mother. Dear Mother ... who spent half her time running the parish—a job she didn't particularly like and wasn't awfully good at—and the other half painting weird Impressionistic pictures and writing long newsy letters to her five children scattered in odd corners of the globe. To all of them, the Rectory was still 'home' and the old ties of love and trust as strong and durable as ever.

She shook her head. 'No, Mrs. Henderson, it's not the same.'

The housekeeper eyed her for a moment and then asked tentatively, 'Is there anything else you want, miss? You've only to ask.'

'Indeed, no!' Fran spoke warmly. 'You've been kindness itself, Mrs. Henderson.' She glanced at her watch. 'Heavens, I'd no idea it was so late! I'd better go and do some unpacking.' (Packing, she recalled with a shudder, had been a nightmare experience, particularly as much of the children's clothing had been damaged in the fire and had had to be replaced. It had all been such a rush. Even now she wasn't sure whether she'd remembered everybody's right size.)

'Well, let me know if there's anything you need.' Mrs. Henderson plodded firmly to the door. Left to herself, Fran moved to the window. Parting the rich plum-coloured curtains, she stood for a moment looking out into the garden, all shimmery and shadowy. The moon shone down on the trunks of the fine old trees and on grass which was so silvered that it glimmered like glass. Somewhere an owl hooted.

It was like something out of a fairy story, Fran thought, then grimaced at herself. She'd be casting herself as the Sleeping Beauty next, and that wasn't much good, since there was no Prince Charming. All the same, it really *was* a marvellous place. She found herself wondering if the unknown 'Mr. Richard' realised what a gem he had inherited. Surely he couldn't be completely indifferent? He didn't deserve his good fortune, she thought indignantly as she drew the curtains again and sniffed the roses on the table before going upstairs to tackle the unpacking.

Inevitably the children were up next day at the proverbial crack of dawn. Since Fran herself woke early, feeling rested and refreshed, she didn't really mind that they all crowded into her room, perching on whatever portion of her bed happened to be readily available.

'I'm hungry,' Danny announced. 'When's breakfast, Fran?'

'Eight o'clock. Not a moment before,' Fran said austerely. She and Mrs. Henderson had made all the necessary arrangements about mealtimes the night before.

Danny sighed. 'I'll *starve* before then. Don't you *care* if I starve?'

'You look a long way off starving,' Fran told him unfeelingly. 'In fact, judging from the weight on my feet, you could do with a diet! Get off, do!' and she rolled over, dislodging Danny so that he fell, a round fat chuckling heap, on to the floor.

'Behave yourself, Danny!' Beanie spoke sternly. Thin and freckled, with straight brown hair cut in a fringe across her forehead, she was a year younger than her brother, but did her best to keep him in order.

Robin wandered over to the window. Usually he was a very silent, self-contained child, but today there was a new eagerness about him which Fran welcomed. 'Can we go out directly we've had breakfast?' he beseeched.

'I don't see why not.' Fran hesitated, remembering Mrs. Henderson's warning. 'You'll be careful in the garden, won't you? It's taken a lot of work to make it as nice as it is, you mustn't do anything to spoil it.'

Robin's face fell and Fran added hastily, 'There are lots of other places where you can play. Mrs. Henderson was telling me last night.'

'There's a squirrel!' Danny had joined Robin at

21

the window.

'Where?' In two huge leaps Mark was across the room. He was crazy about animals.

'It's gone,' Danny said disappointedly. 'Oh, Fran, *please* can we get up now? It *must* be eight o'clock, I just know it must!'

Fran laughed and looked at her watch again. 'It probably will be by the time you're all washed and dressed,' she agreed. It wasn't, it was only a quarter to, but the sounds coming from the kitchen were promising, and sure enough when they trooped through the door breakfast was on the table and Mrs. Henderson, wearing a pretty flowered overall, was beaming at them benevolently.

'We'd better say half-past seven tomorrow, hadn't we?' she said smilingly to Fran. 'Did you sleep well, ducks?' to Danny, who had already seated himself at the table.

'Yes, thanks,' said Danny. He smiled angelically, a Raphael cherub in modern dress. 'Can we start, please?'

'Danny!' Fran exclaimed, but Mrs. Henderson only laughed.

'Hungry, are they? Well, it's a good thing I knew what to expect!' she said, doling out huge plates of porridge.

She was obviously of the opinion that it was advisable to start the day with a solid foundation, but with the exception of Danny the children were too excited to eat much, eager as they were to explore this exciting new world. They gulped down the necessary minimum of food, then sat with their eyes fixed imploringly on Fran, waiting for permission to get down.

'If you'll just give me a hand with the washing up I'll see to everything else,' Mrs. Henderson said cheerfully. 'The children can play in the garden for a few minutes until you're ready to go out. Mind, don't trample on the flowerbeds!' she added, shaking a warning forefinger at the eager faces. 'Sam will be here soon and if he catches you doing what you didn't ought to he'll paddle your bottoms!'

Fran laughed as she began stacking up the dirty crockery. 'He sounds a bit of an ogre!'

'He's not so bad, really, but 'tis no good saying that he's used to children, for he's not.' Mrs. Henderson began operations at the sink as the children, their eyes sparkling, rushed excitedly out into the garden. Danny, though the last to finish eating, as usual led the way.

'Look after Sue, Beanie!' Fran called out after them. Not that Sue needed much looking after. At three, she was much the easiest member of the family to manage, fat and comfortable and placid and un-demanding. It was obvious that she had already won Mrs. Henderson's heart: a little girl, she had told Fran, was what she had always wanted.

From the big window she and Fran watched, smil-ing, as the children scampered on to the big lawn. What must they feel like, Fran wondered, with so much space to play in? The garden at No. 17 had been pocket-handkerchief sized: it had been a small (and welcome) patch of green and that was about all that could be said for it.

'I think they're going to be happy here, don't you?' Mrs. Henderson seemed to read her thoughts.

'I *know* they're happy,' Fran said warmly. It was funny how sometimes good things came out of bad. When the fire had first happened she'd thought it was an utter disaster, but if it hadn't happened then the children would never have had the chance of this heaven-sent holiday. When they'd been here a bit longer, she decided, she'd write and tell Margot Eliot just how much her kindness was being appreciated. She smiled a little ruefully. Strictly speaking, of course, it was not she who was their benefactor but the unknown 'Mr. Richard', though it was patently obvious that he couldn't care less *what* happened to his house or who lived in it!

The next few days passed quickly and pleasantly. The weather was good, so that the children were able to be outdoors all the time. It was their first experience of country life and it seemed as if every day held some new excitement. Fran, watching their sheer radiant happiness, rejoiced. She herself had fallen head over heels in love with Brocade ... it was such a beautiful old house, and it could be made into a marvellous home! If 'Mr. Richard' didn't want it, why didn't he sell it? Presumably because it had been in his family for generations, but it was so silly, keeping a great house standing empty for months on end! Unfair, too.

She felt so strongly about it that when at the end of their first week Margot Eliot paid them an unexpected visit—'I'm attending a weekend conference at Cheltenham and thought I'd drive over to make sure you're settling down all right' she said, smiling—she nearly voiced her opinions aloud. It was a pity, she thought, that the house hadn't been left to Margot, for she was obviously very fond of it.

In her mid-thirties, she was dark and vivacious, with an infectious laugh and a quick, animated way of talking. Fran liked her from the moment she first saw her and was to find that they had quite a lot in common. Like Fran, Margot had done a degree course in social science followed by a twelve-month Child Care course: she had intended to become a Child Care Officer but had married a doctor instead. Fran's lips twisted a little when she heard this, for it was while she was at Sussex University that she had met Bryan, who was reading history. And it was because Bryan had been so impatient for marriage that instead of becoming a Child Care Officer at the end of her course she had applied for a temporary position as a housemother. Then, after Bryan's defection, she had stayed on, finding a certain solace in the fact that at least the children loved and needed her even if Bryan did not.

The children were out when Margot arrived—they had all been invited to tea at a neighbouring farm—and Mrs. Henderson insisted on bringing tea to her and to Fran in the drawing room. Privately Fran thought that this was a mistake and that the small sitting room would have been far cosier, but that was before she realised that the windows had been opened wide to the sunshine and bowls of flowers placed on window-sills and tables. It was amazing how so little effected such a complete transformation. Suddenly the whole room, which had chilled and saddened her a little when she first saw it, became gracious, warm, glowing and altogether welcoming.

After Mrs. Henderson had cleared away the silver tea service and exquisite china Margot relaxed in her chair with a sigh of content. She looked around the room as though satisfying herself that all was as how she remembered it—the priceless Aubusson carpet, the Louis XV chairs and the rare and beautiful pictures on the walls—but her gaze lingered longest on Fran, sitting by the window with the sunlight on her hair.

'Be thankful you're here at Brocade in the summer,' she said smilingly. 'It's the coldest and draughtiest house imaginable in winter! We tried to persuade Uncle to instal central heating, but I'm afraid he fought tooth and nail against anything that smacked of progress! I hope you don't find that the lack of modern conveniences makes things too difficult for you?'

'Oh *no*!' Fran exclaimed. 'I—I love the house. It's absolutely perfect the way it is!'

'That's rather the way I feel,' Margot admitted. 'I used to come and stay here, occasionally, as a child. Never for very long, but I thought it was Paradise, after our town house.'

'That's exactly how we feel,' Fran assured her.

There was a little silence. The faraway look in Margot's eyes seemed to indicate that she was back in the childhood days of which she had spoken, then she roused herself with a little shake.

'My uncle didn't like children, I'm afraid.' She gave a sigh. 'I was absolutely terrified of him when I was small, though because I was rather quiet and shy he never really minded my being here.' Her lips curved into a rueful smile. 'Richard was a different proposition! The only time he ever came here he set the whole house by the ears!'

'Richard?' Fran looked at her, startled. 'You mean your cousin? The new owner?'

Margot nodded. 'Yes. Richard Quayle. He's only lived in South Africa since he was about sixteen, you know. His father died and his mother's second husband was a South African businessman. Before that they lived in Hampshire. Richard must have been— let me see, about twelve—when he spent a holiday here, at the same time as me.' She laughed reminiscently. 'Shall I *ever* forget it? He was always in some kind of hot water! Yet the funny thing was that I think Uncle rather liked him, in spite of everything. He certainly never forgot him—hence his decision to leave him Brocade. I'm selfish enough to feel sorry— I'd have loved it to have been mine.'

'It's a shame!' Fran said indignantly. 'It ought to have been yours! It—it needs to be loved, not neglected! Couldn't you buy it, if your cousin doesn't want it?' She stopped, aghast at her own temerity.

Margot laughed, albeit a little ruefully. 'My dear, it's just as well Uncle didn't leave it to me, because heaven knows how we'd have been able to keep it up! It eats money, you know: it nearly beggared poor Uncle Antony and in the end he had to let an awful lot slide. No, even if Richard offered me Brocade on a plate the sensible thing to do would be to refuse.'

'But if he doesn't want it——'

Margot shrugged. 'As far as anyone knows he *does* want it! If he decided to come back to England to live I don't suppose for a moment it would present any great problems for him: his firm has a branch in London as well as in Johannesburg.' She sighed again. Almost as if speaking to herself she added, 'I haven't seen him for years, but I believe he's become very successful—and very prosperous. I'm not surprised. I've got friends in Johannesburg and from what I hear he's a lot like Uncle Antony. The same ruthless streak. Uncle was as hard as nails and apparently Richard is, too.'

She leant back in her chair, her dark eyes suddenly bright with mischief. 'I wonder just what he'd say if he knew that without so much as a "by your leave" I'd turned Brocade over to you and five children in care? He'd probably be absolutely furious, but luckily he need never know! He's going to give me notice of his homecoming—*if* he ever comes! That's only for his convenience, of course: he'll probably require a gargantuan staff, though where it will come from I haven't the remotest idea! It's an absolute miracle as it is that neither Mrs. Henderson nor Sam has been lured away by more enticing offers!'

Fran laughed, and Margot, looking at her, thought what an attractive girl she was. In fact, she was more than attractive, she was quite lovely, with that very fair hair and those grey-green eyes which were as clear as water. Somehow she fitted in well at Brocade ... she looked at home. But what on earth had prompted a girl like that to devote her life to the really rather thankless task of looking after somebody else's neglected children?

Before she could speak there was the sound of scampering footsteps, followed by shrill, eager voices, and Fran looked up with a smile.

'That must be the children back from the farm. You'll say hello to them before you go back to Cheltenham, won't you?'

'I'd love to,' Margot said, and found that she really meant it. It wasn't until she'd heard the children's voices and the sound of their laughter that she'd suddenly realised what Brocade had lacked ever since she'd known it. Children's laughter, in this old house, was a more daring innovation than even central heating would have been!

CHAPTER THREE

THE August weather continued marvellous and for the most part the children were reasonably good. Fran and Mrs. Henderson had become firm friends, for Fran allowed the elder woman to 'mother' them all and never tried to interfere in domestic matters. Mrs. Henderson's pride permitted her only to make the beds, help with the washing up and mind the children, so consequently she had more freedom than she had had for many months and she made the most of it.

The only real cloud on the horizon appeared when a short letter came from Miss Challoner. Her news was not good: Pauline, always moody and difficult, was proving a headache for her new housemother, and the condition of Danny's and Beanie's mother had deteriorated. Her chances of eventual recovery now seemed slim indeed, and Fran's face was sober as she folded the letter up and replaced it in its envelope. She looked across the table to where the two children were sitting and sighed. Poor Danny ... poor Beanie! What did the future hold for them if their mother died? Adoption, probably ... they were delightful children, suitable in every way. But adoption would almost certainly mean separation, and they were a devoted brother and sister.

Mrs. Henderson's voice broke in on her troubled thoughts. She too had received a letter this morning and judging from her expression it contained welcome news.

'It's from my Johnny,' she explained. 'He's written to say that he's got a business call to make in this area and he's going to try to make time to pop in and see me. I'm that pleased! I haven't seen hair or hide of him for the past four or five months, been too busy, he says.'

'Oh, that's nice!' Fran said warmly. She knew that Johnny, the youngest of Mrs. Henderson's five sons, was also the apple of her eye. He had, to quote his proud mother, 'done well for himself'. He had won a scholarship to Oxford and with a B.A. to his credit was at present taking his Ph.D. Like most students, however, during the long vacation he was glad of a job and was at present selling encyclopaedias. 'When is he coming?'

The question was never answered, for just at that moment there was an outraged wail from Beanie.

'Fran! Mark's taking all the sugar!'

Fran looked, saw that Mark was indeed trying to empty the contents of the sugar basin on to his porridge, and leant over and removed it from his hand.

'Don't be greedy, Mark. Besides, too much sugar is bad for you,' she said severely.

'It tastes nice,' said Mark, unrepentant, and scowled at Beanie. 'You're an old tell-tale, Beanie!'

Indignant tears sprang into Beanie's eyes. 'I'm not! I'm not a tell-tale! But if I hadn't said anything there wouldn't have been any sugar left for Danny!'

'If you make Beanie cry I'll thump you,' Danny said pugnaciously.

'Boys!' Fran hastily intervened to pour oil on troubled waters, and for a few moments there was silence.

'I haven't got enough milk.' Robin was the next to voice a grievance. Without taking his eyes off his porridge Danny reached rudely across Mark for the milk and banged it down before Robin with such vigour that it slopped over on to the clean tablecloth.

'Danny, be careful!' Fran said sharply.

'Don't like porridge,' Sue said distinctly, and

pushed her plate away from her just as Mrs. Henderson was mopping up the spilt milk. Her elbow sent the plate flying, with the result that a liberal portion of porridge bespattered wall and floor.

'Crash!' said Sue with interest, and the other children dissolved into helpless giggles.

Mrs. Henderson and Fran glanced meaningly at each other. It's going to be one of Those Days, thought Fran, and she was right, for after that troubles came thick and fast. Robin fell down some stone steps and loosened a front tooth. Sue was sick—having sucked the paint off a gaudily-coloured wooden engine of suspect origins—and Beanie lost a treasured 'lucky' sixpence for which the entire household was required to seek high and low. Mark climbed on to a shed and hurt his foot jumping off and at lunchtime Danny tore his new jersey on a nail in the trellis. Repairing it so that the damage would not be too noticeable was obviously going to be a major task, and with a sigh Fran, who hated darning, resigned herself to an afternoon spent with needle and thread. The children had elected to play cowboys and Red Indians in the little copse which was one of their favourite haunts, and Fran went with them, feeling that since it was so warm and sunny she might just as well work outside as indoors.

She had finished the darn, and was leaning back against an ivy-covered tree, relaxed in a happy dream, when a sudden scream of terror made her spring to her feet, her rainbow fancies fallen into cureless ruin.

'Help! Oh, Fran, help!' That was unmistakably Robin's voice, and Fran looked round wildly. Then she caught a glimpse of Beanie's red cotton frock through the trees and raced madly in that direction as the cries for help grew louder and more urgent.

Beanie came running to meet her, white to the lips. 'Fran, Danny's stuck in a tree! He can't get down!'

31

Oh, help him!' she sobbed.

At the bottom of a big tree with spreading branches Mark, Robin and little Sue were gazing upwards with frightened faces.

'The branch is bending!' Mark said hoarsely. 'Look, it's going to break!'

Beanie began to sob more loudly than ever. Danny was clinging on for dear life to a slender branch which was indeed bending ominously under his weight. Fran caught her breath. If he fell from that height he could hurt himself badly!

She groaned aloud. 'How many times have I told you children *not* to climb trees unless I'm with you?'

Danny heard her voice. 'Get me down! Get me down! I'm stuck!' he wailed.

'It's my fault.' Mark's voice was scared. 'I dared him.'

There was no time to waste on reproaches. It was impossible, Fran realised, for her to climb up after Danny, for none of the branches around him would bear the weight of an adult person. The child's only hope was to keep absolutely still: if he moved then the bough would surely break.

She spoke quickly, trying to sound as reassuring as she could. 'Danny, whatever you do you must keep quite, quite still. If you do then you'll be all right. Promise you won't move?'

'Y-yes,' Danny quavered.

'Good boy! Now I'm going to find Sam just as quickly as I can and he'll bring a big ladder. We'll get you down in no time. Remember, keep still!'

'All right.' Danny sounded perilously close to tears, but Fran knew that he could be trusted to obey instructions. She thought rapidly. In actual fact she wasn't sure where Sam was working: she might waste precious moments looking for him. But she knew where the ladder was kept—behind the potting shed

—and Mrs. Henderson would surely help her to carry it!

Her mind made up, she ran like the wind towards the house. Outside the front door a long, silver-grey car was standing: she did not check her headlong flight, but wondered to whom it belonged and if the owner could help in this present emergency. Mrs. Eliot? No, her car was red. Then she remembered what Mrs. Henderson had told her at breakfast that morning and gave a gasp of relief. Perhaps Johnny Henderson was here! A brawny young man was just what she needed!

She ran into the house. Mrs. Henderson was not in the kitchen, but a man was standing by the open library door—a tall, broad-shouldered man with a lean, deeply tanned face and grey eyes. Not that Fran really took in the details of his appearance: she was too relieved that her surmise had been correct. This man was looking so much at home that he couldn't possibly be anyone but Johnny Henderson.

'Oh, please, can you come quickly?' she asked breathlessly. 'There's a little boy stuck in a tree in the copse—he can't get down and I'm terrified that the branch is going to break at any moment! I know where there's a ladder, but I can't carry it by myself, it's too heavy!'

In her anxiety she did not notice the expression of blank surprise that spread over the man's face, but he wasted no time on unnecessary words.

'Tell me where to find the ladder: I'll manage it alone. Get back to the child and make sure he doesn't do anything silly,' he said curtly, and with a sob of thankfulness Fran obeyed.

She ran as fast as she could, but she was hampered by an agonising stitch in her side, so that Johnny Henderson, shouldering the heavy ladder with perfect ease, was not so far behind her when she burst into the copse. To her immeasurable relief the children were still grouped around the tree, shouting encouragement to Danny who was clinging desperately on to the slender branch with arms and knees.

'Haven't you brought a ladder?' Mark caught hold of her arm, alarm written across his face. 'He says he doesn't think he can hold on much longer!'

'Don't worry, it's coming! Hold on, Danny! You'll soon be down now!' she called up into the tree.

No sooner had she spoken than Johnny Henderson was beside her.

'Stand back, all of you!' The brusque order was instantly obeyed, Fran and the children watching in silent suspense as quickly but carefully he set the ladder against the trunk and shinned up. On reaching the top he took a quick look round, then hoisted himself on to a branch which looked slightly thicker than the others though it creaked protestingly, and stretched out his right arm. Balancing himself so precariously that Fran felt almost sick with apprehension, he grabbed hold of Danny's clothing.

'All right, I've got you!' His calm voice was infinitely reassuring to the frightened child. 'Slowly edge your way backwards. You won't fall; I won't let you.'

Only Fran realised that if the branch broke and Danny *did* fall his weight would drag the man off his perch and hurl him backwards. She watched, white-faced, as little by little Danny moved back along the branch. He was nearly at the end when it gave an ominous crack.

'Oh, it's going to break!' Beanie shouted in an agony of terror, but even as the branch gave way with a crash Johnny Henderson had seized the child around the middle and with a tremendous effort had regained his footing on the ladder. For a moment it swayed precariously under the double burden, then the man steadied himself and hoisted Danny across his broad shoulders, fireman's style. A sigh of relief went up from the children as slowly he descended the ladder and swung Danny on to the ground.

'Danny!' Half crying, half laughing, Beanie rushed forward to fling her arms round her brother, and in a moment he was the centre of an eager jostling group. Fran, having first satisfied herself that the child was none the worse for his adventure, turned gratefully to his rescuer. Screwing up her eyes against the golden dazzle of the sunshine, she really looked at him for the first time. Tall and undeniably good-looking, he held himself well, with a sort of easy, well-knit movement that spoke of perfect physical fitness. It puzzled her a little that although his features—black brows, straight nose, hard mouth and strong chin—bore not the slightest resemblance to his mother's, she could not rid herself of the conviction that she had seen him somewhere before.

She began to stammer her thanks, but he cut her short almost rudely.

'Perhaps,' he said harshly, 'you'll kindly explain why these children are trespassing on private land?'

'Trespassing?' Fran stared at him, momentarily taken aback. Heavens, hadn't his mother told him? 'Oh, but we're not! It's quite all right, really it is! We're staying at Brocade, didn't you know?'

'It's our new home,' Mark explained. 'Our old one got burned.' He pressed close to Johnny Henderson's side, filled with admiration for the way in which this splendid being had plucked Danny out of the tree and carried him to safety. It was, he thought, just what his father would have done. Not that he could actually remember his father ... but it was inconceivable that he could be anything but strong and brave and resourceful like this tall stranger.

'We're going to stay here for ever and for ever!' Beanie proclaimed shrilly. She so much wanted this to happen that she had almost come to believe it. She seized hold of Johnny Henderson's hand and looked confidingly up into his face. 'I do like you! Will you come to tea?'

'Beanie!' Fran remonstrated, laughing, but as she met Johnny Henderson's cold grey eyes and saw the way in which he brushed Beanie aside the laugh died on her lips. He was looking at her intently, and she found his close unwavering regard oddly disconcerting. There was a moment's uncomfortable silence, then the man drew a long breath, a deep crease gathering between his brows.

'It seems,' he said icily, 'that someone has been taking one hell of a liberty with what I've reason to believe is *my* property. I suppose you consider that an absentee owner is fair game, but——'

He stopped short as Fran let out an involuntary gasp. 'My' property? An incredible and dreadful premonition seized her and her hand went instinctively to her cheek. Oh, why had she jumped to such rash conclusions? This wasn't Johnny Henderson! Dark brows, strong chin, firmly closed lips ... this was the younger, living counterpart of the portrait in the library! *Now* she knew why that brown face had seemed strangely familiar!

'Oh, good heavens!' she said, aghast. 'Are you ... can you be...?'

His eyes were like a winter sky and his voice was inimical. 'I am Richard Quayle. Brocade belongs to me—unless, of course, you've planned a permanent take-over?' he added, very politely.

Fran was scarlet with mortification. What an impossible, embarrassing situation! She said breathlessly, 'Look, I know it must seem odd, our being here, but I can explain. You see, our house really was badly burned and there was nowhere else for us to go, so——'

He cut her short. 'Spare me the sob story. I'm not interested.' Then, as she stiffened, 'What I want to know is how long have you been here? Who gave you permission to come?' He looked from her to the children. Almost frighteningly sensitive to atmosphere, instinctively they had drawn together, realising but not comprehending the man's unfriendliness. 'And where's your husband?'

For the second time Fran was knocked off balance. 'My hus——? But I'm not married!' She saw his dark brows lift a fraction and was annoyed to feel herself blushing more furiously than ever. 'These children aren't mine! I mean, they are, but——' She stopped, looking helplessly round at the circle of solemn young faces. There was bewilderment in their eyes, and at the sight of it she felt a sudden rush of indignation. Poor babes, they weren't going to be embroiled in this if she could help it! Richard Quayle would just have to wait for his explanation!

Lifting her chin, she looked at him and said, with a coldness which matched his, 'The children are tired and upset. May we please talk about this later?'

Richard Quayle stuck his hands into his pockets and she realised with a sudden jolt that although he was obviously holding himself in careful check he was furiously angry. Even so, she was totally unprepared for his next words.

'No, we may not. As far as I'm concerned there is nothing to talk about. You are trespassers in my home and I must ask you to pack and leave. Immediately.'

For a moment Fran was too stunned to answer him. She stared at him, her face slowly whitening. Then Robin, grasping the situation quicker than the rest and realising the threat to his new-found security, burst into anguished tears and Beanie, suffering from reaction, promptly followed suit.

'Children, don't cry!' Fran whirled round to comfort them. Her arms around them, she turned her head to look at Richard Quayle, her eyes blazing with anger. How dared he give such an order without first

37

bothering to hear their side of the story? Margot Eliot had talked about a ruthless streak, but she'd said nothing about sheer blazing arrogance!

'I hope you're satisfied! Oh, go away, you—you bully!' she choked.

Furious at somehow having been placed in the wrong although he felt himself to be so obviously in the right, Richard Quayle stood staring at her and the sobbing children, a slow flush creeping up under his deep tan. Then as Sue joined the woeful chorus he gave a smothered exclamation, turned on his heel and strode away in the direction of the house.

Fran could feel Robin's thin body quivering beneath her hands. 'Why is that man angry with us? Why have we got to go away?'

'Is it because I climbed the tree?' There was a catch in Danny's breath. 'I—I didn't have a chance to say thank you.'

'It wasn't your fault. Don't worry about that.' Fran reassured him quickly, but her thoughts were chaotic. Richard Quayle had meant what he said. There was no doubt about that whatsoever. Even when he eventually learned how they came to be here it was unlikely to make the slightest difference. He did not want them at Brocade. He had made that abundantly clear. 'Pack and leave. Immediately.' She bit her lip as she recalled his peremptory words. He surely hadn't meant them to be taken absolutely literally? Oh, he was within his rights, of course, but where on earth could they go to at this time of day? Desperately she tugged at her hair and tried to think. Perhaps the best thing to do was to get in touch with Margot Eliot. After all, it was she who was really responsible for this frightful situation! She had been so sure that Richard Quayle would not come home to claim his inheritance without giving her due warning!

'Oh, *drat* the man!' she thought savagely. Why hadn't he done just that? Why had he come home so unexpectedly? And why, oh, why did he have to be such a thoroughly unpleasant character? 'I wouldn't *want* to stay here now, after the way he's behaved!' she told herself indignantly, then she glanced at the children's unhappy, tear-streaked faces and her conscience smote her. It was far, far worse for them than it was for her!

It was a very subdued little group which trailed back to the house. Much to Fran's relief, there was no sign of Richard Quayle, but Mrs. Henderson was in the kitchen and one look at her plump, rosy face was enough to tell Fran that she was very much put out. Her lips were tightly compressed and there was a decidedly militant sparkle in her black eyes. It did not require great psychic powers to guess that she too had made the acquaintance of the new master of Brocade and that whatever had ensued at that meeting had not been to her liking. Nevertheless, tea was laid as usual—nothing, not even an earthquake, was likely to cause Mrs. Henderson to deviate from her customary clockwork routine—and at the sight of new scones, spread with farm butter and home-made strawberry jam, and their favourite chocolate biscuits, the children's spirits lifted. Fran waited until they were all munching happily, then turned to the housekeeper and spoke in a low voice.

'You've seen Mr. Quayle?' It was a statement more than a question.

'I have.' Mrs. Henderson smacked down a cup and saucer with such force that the draining board rattled. She paused, then added grimly, 'He told me what happened. Danny's all right, I'm glad to see. It doesn't seem to have affected his appetite, does it?'

'No.' Fran smiled wanly, then brushed her hand across her eyes. 'I was so stupid. I—I thought he was your Johnny. He was here, you see, when I came in and—and it seemed a natural conclusion. Where were you, by the way?'

'I'd just popped down to the village for those dratted biscuits.' Mrs. Henderson nodded towards the tea table. 'I wasn't gone more than ten minutes, but bless me if His Lordship didn't have to come and walk into an empty house!' She sniffed and added belligerently, 'Not that he had any right to expect much else, when he hadn't even taken the trouble to let anyone know he was coming!'

Fran drew a long quivering breath. 'I suppose in one way it was lucky he was here. I couldn't have got Danny down from that tree by myself. Oh, didn't he tell you that he'd rescued Danny?' as the housekeeper's face registered surprise.

'No. Just that he'd met you and five children and that one of them was stuck in a tree. He had other things on his mind,' Mrs. Henderson said significantly.

Fran bit her lip. 'He—he was frightfully angry when I said we were staying here. He wouldn't listen when I tried to explain that his cousin had invited us.'

'*I* made him listen!' Mrs. Henderson's eyes snapped at the memory. 'He seemed to think it was a put-up job between us, until I told him different! Took the wind out of his sails, too, it did. I reckon he's telephoning Mrs. Eliot now; he asked for her number.' She picked up the heavy teapot and began pouring tea for Fran and herself. 'A nice homecoming and no mistake! He's a tartar, if ever I saw one!'

'Don't I know it!' Fran gave a rueful laugh. She paused, then added shamefacedly, 'I—I rather think I called him a bully.' She had regretted that flash of temper ever since: it had been undignified to say the least of it. And very unwise.

'You never?' Mrs. Henderson stared at her openmouthed.

'He told me to pack our things and go. The children heard him and they cried,' Fran said simply. Her face set in anxious lines. 'Mrs. Henderson, he surely *can't* expect us to go tonight! There's nowhere for us to stay!'

Mrs. Henderson placed her hands on her hips. She was breathing fast, but what she would have said Fran never knew, for just at that moment a bell rang, sounding shrill and peremptory.

'That's him.' Mrs. Henderson unfastened her apron and began waddling to the door. The light of battle was in her eyes, but Fran, seizing the opportunity to coax Sue to drink her milk, did not see it. She had yet to learn that Mrs. Henderson, when roused, could be a formidable adversary.

Tea was always the meal that the children liked best and it was invariably a noisy occasion, but to-night, though they did full justice to the food, they were much quieter than usual. Fran, dreading the questions they were bound to ask and the decision that soon must be taken, did her best to appear completely normal, but it was uphill work and she was thankful when after a few minutes Mrs. Henderson reappeared. She was more flushed than Fran had ever seen her, but she had the look of a woman who had done her duty.

'He wants to see you. Never mind about the children, I'll see to them,' she said shortly.

Fran ran her tongue round suddenly dry lips and smoothed her hair with a quick nervous gesture. It was with her heart beating unaccountably fast that she crossed the big entrance hall and tapped lightly on the library door, which was ajar.

'Come in.'

Richard Quayle was standing by the fireplace, glancing through a book. He looked up as Fran entered, and the resemblance between him and the portrait above his head struck her with irresistible force. It was not just that their features were so similar, it was their expressions too. If old Sir Antony had been granite, this man was steel.

41

Now that she no longer saw him through a dazzle of sunlight, Fran realised that he was older than she had at first supposed. Life had brought Sir Antony power and riches, but also disillusionment and unhappiness, and the same story was etched in his nephew's hollowed temples, the dark stains beneath his eyes and the suggestion of bitterness about his mouth.

He shut the book he was holding and laid it down. He said coldly, 'Sit down, won't you?' and though she had been prepared for it the unfriendliness in his eyes almost shocked her.

She opened her mouth to speak, but he forestalled her.

'Apparently I owe you an apology, inasmuch as you are not trespassers, as I thought, but invited guests. I have just been speaking to my cousin on the telephone and she has made the situation abundantly clear.' He paused, and Fran, completely at a loss for perhaps the first time in her life, murmured something inaudible. Not that it mattered, for he continued as though she had not spoken.

'The fact that she had no authority whatsoever to invite you and half a dozen waifs and strays to take up your abode at Brocade appears to her to be entirely irrelevant.' His voice was flat and hard. 'She insists that she gave an undertaking that you and the children could stay here at Brocade until your own home was again fit for habitation and I gather that she expects me to honour that undertaking.' He frowned, not looking at her, and Fran's eyes widened. What was he trying to say?

'After due deliberation I have decided to do so.' There was no mistaking the reluctance in his voice and Fran, who had given an incredulous gasp, felt the colour flood into her cheeks. 'Not,' he added deliberately, 'that I feel in any way obliged to do so, nor need you flatter yourself that I feel the slightest sympathy for your plight. I have never pretended to have philanthropic leanings. My only reason for allowing you to remain at Brocade is, quite frankly, that I have no wish to embarrass my cousin, however much she may deserve it. Also'—and here his voice became even grimmer—'you appear to have found a powerful ally in Mrs. Henderson. She has left me in no doubt that if you and the children are forced to leave, she will leave also—and though I could almost certainly find another housekeeper just as efficient, that might take time, and I don't have too much of that commodity to spare.'

Fran was white now. 'I can assure you that we have no desire to stay on at Brocade as unwelcome guests! Directly we can find alternative accommodation we shall leave!'

'How very obliging of you.' Richard Quayle answered her coolly, a faintly mocking glint in his grey eyes. 'I am glad we are of the same mind. I shall not, of course, make the slightest attempt to disabuse you of the notion that you are "unwelcome" guests. Just as you are entitled to think of me as a bully, so am I entitled to think of you as an unmitigated nuisance. I came here expecting peace and quiet. I don't like children at the best of times, and the thought of sharing a house with five of them—even a house as big as this one—is utterly unpalatable. I shall expect you to ensure that they are kept out of my way as much as possible.'

'You needn't worry about that!' Fran almost flung the words at him.

'I hope you are right. Frankly, I think you are rather too young to exercise proper control over so many children. What happened this afternoon appears to bear that out.'

He picked up his book as if to signify that the interview was at an end. Fran, flaming with resentment at the unfairness of his last thrust, could not have trusted herself to speak even if she had wanted to.

43

She had never been so angry in all her life—and never, she told herself passionately as she left the library, had she ever disliked anyone as much as she now disliked the owner of Brocade!

CHAPTER FOUR

For the first time since she had come to Brocade Fran slept badly. The thought of being the unwanted guests of a man as detestable as Richard Quayle haunted her, but though she tossed and turned nearly all night she could see no way out of what seemed an impossible situation. She had telephoned Miss Challoner immediately after her stormy interview with Richard Quayle and had begged for permission to return to London, but after she had reluctantly admitted that they were not, in fact, being turned out Miss Challoner's attitude had been definitely unsympathetic.

It was, she told Fran, a pity that Richard Quayle had unexpectedly returned, but since he had agreed to their remaining at Brocade what was there to worry about? All she had to do was to see that the children behaved themselves and that their presence did not obtrude. When Fran had persisted that she would rather not stay at Brocade under the present circumstances Miss Challoner had snapped back that surely she had not forgotten that there was always a desperate shortage of beds? She added, tartly, that she had just spent the whole day desperately trying to find accommodation for a family of seven whose mother had deserted them and that she saw no reason to add to her problems unnecessarily!

The children, of course, were overjoyed to learn that after all they were not to leave Brocade. Fran impressed upon them that they would have to be careful to make no noise, and they assured her fervently that they would be as quiet as mice. Perhaps, she tried to comfort herself, they could manage to live under the same roof as Richard Quayle and yet see nothing of him. They always spent as much time as possible out of doors and Mrs. Henderson had prepared him a handsome room in the west wing, as far away from Fran's and the children's rooms as possible.

What his plans were, and whether he intended to stay long at Brocade, nobody seemed to know. Certainly the intense interest that he took in every aspect of his inheritance seemed to indicate that this was his intention. Armed with a notebook and pencil, he made a thorough inspection of both house and garden and both Mrs. Henderson and Sam were kept constantly on the hop. He found no fault with either, but, the housekeeper told Fran, he had the eyes of a lynx and nothing—be it a broken tile, a tree that need pruning, or a picture that needed cleaning—escaped his notice. The almost total lack of modern amenities did not appear to meet with his approval and Mrs. Henderson thought that he probably intended to make sweeping changes. Even though she told herself that it was none of her business Fran could not help feeling rather dismayed, for she believed she knew the kind of changes Richard Quayle would make. A man like him, she thought bitterly, was unlikely to appreciate the fact that Brocade belonged in spirit to another century.

He had given Mrs. Henderson orders to open up all the dark and shrouded rooms, but no sooner had these instructions been given than he had rushed off to London, giving no indication when he would be back. Fran learnt of his departure with real relief: she had been living in a state of acute nervous tension for the past three days and was thankful that she need no longer keep a sharp look out for possible trouble. Their paths had not crossed, but that was merely due to a combination of careful planning and sheer good luck—and the latter was not likely to last for ever!

While he was away there was a telephone call from Margot Eliot. Her cousin's unexpected arrival—due, apparently, to the sudden death of the man in charge of the London branch of his firm—had obviously been as much of a shock to her as it had been to everyone else. Now that her initial dismay had subsided, however, she was inclined to make light of Fran's misgivings.

'You feel like intruders? Nonsense, my dear!' she said cheerfully. 'Oh, I admit Richard *was* a bit peeved to find that I'd installed you without so much as a by-your-leave, but as I told him, in a place the size of Brocade you could live with a dozen kids and hardly know they were there!' Then, as Fran demurred, she added, 'Just keep them out of his hair and everything will be fine!'

Which was all very well, Fran thought ruefully as she replaced the receiver, but just how could she guarantee to do that?

'Well, it's no good meeting trouble half-way,' Mrs. Henderson told her briskly. Although she was still quite prepared to champion Fran and the children if the need arose, her own opinion of the new master of Brocade had undergone a favourable change in the last few days. There'd been that initial misunderstanding, but after that he'd treated her with every consideration, and Sam too. He certainly wasn't as ready with a smile or a laugh as he might be, but things could be worse ... a lot worse.

'Count your blessings, that's what I do,' she advised.

Fran laughed, then sighed. Usually she didn't need to be reminded to count her blessings. But perhaps Mrs. Henderson couldn't be expected to understand how much she hated being the recipient of a grudging hospitality!

During Richard Quayle's absence in London Johnny Henderson paid his promised visit to Brocade.

He was a tall, loosely-knit young man with merry

47

blue eyes and pleasant if undistinguished features. He was, Fran thought, quite a lot like his mother, not only physically but in temperament also. He had her kindheartedness and her plain common sense, the last quality leavened, in his case, by a twinkling sense of humour. He was a little shy with Fran, but quickly endeared himself to the children, who were enchanted to discover a grown-up whose energy and amiability seemed boundless.

'I wish he were a permanency here!' Fran laughed to his mother after he had departed. 'He'd be a tremendous asset, wouldn't he?'

'He's always been fond of children. He used to help run a Cub pack at one time,' Mrs. Henderson said, gratified.

She sighed a little. During a few moments alone with Johnny he had told her that he was thinking of getting married. It had to happen some day, of course, but she wished he would wait, at any rate until he'd left Oxford. She could only hope he had chosen wisely. Someone like Fran, for instance—so bright and gay and pretty, yet such a fine 'mother' and homemaker.

She was so busy wondering what her future daughter-in-law would be like that for once she was absent-minded, with the result that there was a domestic disaster involving a cold chicken, a jug of cream and a tabby cat named Matilda. Though it had really been her own fault for leaving the pantry door open she was full of righteous indignation.

'That dratted cat!' she said bitterly. 'Just wait till the next time I set eyes on her! I'll show her what's what, the thieving animal!'

Fran, who had a soft spot for cats, sought to pour oil on troubled waters. 'Well, she *has* got seven kittens to feed!'

Mrs. Henderson snorted. Matilda had indeed recently produced seven kittens, three black and white and four exact replicas of herself, in a basket prepared for that very purpose. The children had seen them when they were only a few hours old and had been enchanted. Matilda, however, might have misinterpreted their cries of delight, for she had removed her progeny to another resting place overnight and no one had been able to find them.

'I don't care how many kittens she's got, that's no excuse for making off with today's dinner! I'd like to know where she's hiding out: those kittens will be too big to drown soon, Sam says.'

In the heat of the moment Mrs. Henderson had forgotten one of her favourite maxims—that little pitchers had ears. A horrified silence greeted her remark. All five children, who were having their 'elevenses'—milk and biscuits—looked at her in stunned disbelief.

'Sam wouldn't *really* drown them? Not those sweet little kittens?' Beanie asked, her eyes round with reproach.

'I wouldn't let him! It's too cruel!' Mark the animal lover cried indignantly, clenching his small brown fists.

'Not cruel at all, ducks, not when they're small,' Mrs. Henderson said firmly. She was not unfeeling, but she had the countrywoman's calm acceptance of life and death. 'What would we do with eight cats, now? They soon grow up, you know, they don't stay kittens for ever.'

'Well, you could find homes for them, couldn't you?' Mark protested, and looked at Fran imploringly. 'I'd *love* one!'

Fran knew only too well what he wanted her to say, but she had to shake her head. Since she had been with the children they had had several dearly-loved pets, including a hamster, a white rabbit, and a tortoise, but cats were 'out' because for some mysterious reason Pauline was allergic to them.

Mark said no more, but his small face was full of

49

determination. Later in the day, when the others were playing with a bat and ball, Fran missed him and after calling his name in vain for several minutes, decided to go in search of him. It would never do if he made himself a nuisance to Sam, who had a deep-rooted antipathy to all small boys.

Mrs. Henderson thought that she had seen him making for the summer house, but when Fran reached it she could see no sign of him. She was about to retrace her footsteps when the sound of a muffled sneeze startled her and she turned swiftly. She was just in time to see Mark sliding cautiously round the south side of the summer house, from the direction of a small potting shed which had fallen into disuse and was scheduled for demolition when Sam had time to see to it.

When Mark saw Fran waiting for him he stopped abruptly and looked the picture of guilt.

'Oh, it's you!' he said lamely.

'Certainly it's me! What have you been up to?' Fran asked suspiciously.

For a moment Mark hesitated, as if searching for an excuse, then he smiled disarmingly. He knew he couldn't pull the wool over Fran's eyes, but he knew equally well that she could be trusted.

'I saw Matilda and I followed her, because I wanted to see where she's hidden her kittens. It's a good place, I don't believe anyone else will ever find it. Shall I show you?'

Fran, intrigued, followed him past the summer house and into the potting shed. The door was half off its hinges, the interior was dusty and cobwebby and smelt rather dank, and it was filled with an odd conglomeration of articles—paint tins, oil drums, rusty tools and a derelict lawn-mower. It did not seem likely that Matilda would have chosen such an un-prepossessing home for her family, but Mark went straight to a corner, where there stood a big box.

'Here they are,' he said.

Fran peered into the box. It was half full of straw, and nestling in the middle were the seven missing kittens, curled together in a sleeping, furry bundle. She put down her hand and touched them gently.

'They've grown, haven't they?' Mark enquired anxiously. 'Matilda will only have to keep them hidden for a little while longer, won't she? Then they'll be too big to drown, Mrs. Henderson said so.' He hesitated again. 'You really won't tell?'

Fran shook her head. 'Of course I won't. I don't want them to be drowned either.' She laughed as Matilda, purring loudly, brushed past them and jumped into the box, hiding her family from view. I don't think we need worry. You're right, it *is* a good hiding place. Sam won't think of looking here.'

But she was wrong. For one more day she and Mark shared Matilda's secret, Mark hugging himself in secret glee whenever he thought how cleverly the little tabby cat was thwarting Sam's evil intentions. Then the blow fell.

Creeping stealthily to the potting shed after breakfast with some titbits he had managed to store away in his pockets for Matilda's benefit, Mark found to his horror and dismay that the box was empty. For a few moments he stood transfixed. Oh, Sam *couldn't* have found them! Matilda herself must have carried them off to yet another hiding place! Then, as if to give the lie to this wild hope, he felt something soft and furry rubbing up against his bare legs, and when he looked down there was Matilda, thin and wraith-like, mewing piteously.

Even then Mark refused to believe that the kittens really had gone for ever. They'd been so small and soft and helpless, surely nobody—not even Sam!— could possibly have hurt them! Or could they? There was only one way to find out. Picking Matilda up in his arms, he ran as fast as his short sturdy legs would carry him to where Sam was working in the kitchen garden. The old man never spoke to the children if he could possibly help it, he merely grunted, but this time Mark was determined to *make* him talk!

Ten minutes later Fran, who was helping Mrs. Henderson with the washing up, looked up in dismay as Mark burst into the kitchen and flung himself on her, sobbing bitterly, his tear-streaked face crimson with grief and anger.

'He's done it! Fran, he's done it! Sam's drowned the kittens!'

'Oh no!' Fran's heart missed a beat. 'Mark, are you sure? How do you know?' She looked over his head at Mrs. Henderson and knew at once, from the expression on the housekeeper's face, that he was not mistaken.

'He told me!' The small shoulders heaved convulsively. 'I went to the potting shed, but the box was empty, and then Matilda came and mewed and mewed and wouldn't stop mewing! So then I knew something was wrong and I went and asked Sam and he said yes, he found them last night and he'd drowned them all. All!' Mark's voice was shrill with despair.

'Oh, Mark, I'm so sorry!' Fran's voice was pitiful as she put her arms round the child and tried to comfort him. Comfort, however, was not what Mark wanted.

'How could he *do* it?' he demanded passionately. 'He's a murderer, that's what he is! They hadn't done him any harm! He's cruel and horrible and I *hate* him, and I just wish somebody would drown *him*!'

Fran took him firmly by the shoulders. 'Now, Mark, Stop it! Sam wasn't cruel.' Fighting back her own revulsion, she tried to explain that the old gardener had thought he was acting for the best, but knew from the child's expression that he was unconvinced. Mark in this mood was difficult to deal with: he could be maddeningly stubborn when he chose.

It was, of course, too much to hope that he would keep his anger and his sorrow to himself. The other children soon knew what had happened and expressed their feelings in their different ways. Beanie wept and Danny enquired anxiously if the kittens had gone to Heaven. Surprisingly, quiet Robin was nearly as angry as Mark.

'It would serve that old Sam right if someone killed *his* children!' he said loudly.

'Don't be silly. He hasn't got any,' said Danny the logical, but a sudden gleam had come into Mark's eyes. It had just occurred to him that the kittens might be avenged.

Fran missed the gleam, but she noticed, and was puzzled by, Mark's subsequent air of suppressed excitement. She had every intention of discovering the reason for it, but before she could do so her attention was distracted by Sue, who started complaining of earache. The little girl had had trouble with her ears since she was a baby and was, indeed, slightly deaf, so that Fran did not feel inclined to take chances. When teatime came and the pain appeared to be worse she decided, after a swift consultation with Mrs. Henderson, to call in the village doctor.

'He's a nice young man, Dr. Coates. He's said to have a way with children even though he's none of his own,' Mrs. Henderson told her. 'He and his wife haven't lived here long. She's a pretty little thing, but keeps herself to herself. I reckon as how she must be lonely, living right at the other end of the village with no friends to speak of. Still, that's her look-out,' and she shrugged her plump shoulders.

Fran liked Dr. Coates on sight. He was a tall young man who moved with a kind of steady patience and he had a gentle mouth which was offset by the firmness of his jaw. He handled Sue with a skill which won her confidence and Fran's admiration, and was able to give an assurance that there was nothing seriously wrong.

'You're the young lady with the five foster-children, aren't you?' he asked Fran smilingly as he prepared to leave. His eyes dwelt thoughtfully on her eager face. Nice girl ... a lovely smile.

Fran met his penetrating gaze with a complete lack of self-consciousness. Her grey-green eyes held an expression of direct and friendly interest tinged with amusement.

'Yes, I am. How did you know about the children?'

'Oh, news travels pretty quickly in a village the size of this.' He paused. 'Are you staying here long?'

'No. It's a temporary arrangement only.' Fran spoke a little too emphatically and a look of disappointment crossed the doctor's face.

'A pity.' He saw the flicker of surprise in her eyes and smiled a little wryly. 'I'm afraid that I was rather hoping you'd befriend my wife. There aren't so many people of her own age hereabouts and she's rather lonely. I'd have very much liked her to meet you.'

'There's no earthly reason why we shouldn't meet. We may be here for several weeks yet.' Fran, her sympathy aroused, spoke quickly. 'Perhaps she'd like to join us for a picnic tea one day? She wouldn't be daunted by the thought of so many children, would she?'

She was only joking, but to her surprise the doctor's face shadowed. For a moment he hesitated, then he said awkwardly, 'Well, that's very nice of you, but what about your coming to dinner with us one evening first? Or do you have baby-sitter problems?'

Frank shook her head and Dr. Coates looked relieved. 'That's fine. I'll tell Rosemary I've met you and perhaps we can fix something soon.'

He was embarrassed about something, Fran thought as he left, and knit her brows. He hadn't been at all enthusiastic about the picnic suggestion—but why? Was Rosemary Coates so sophisticated that that kind of thing didn't appeal? If so, then no wonder that she was having difficulty in making friends! Mrs. Henderson had as good as said that she was standoffish, and that was a pity, when her husband was so nice and unassuming!

Sue was ready for sleep. Fran tucked her up and kissed her goodnight, then went downstairs to round up the rest of her brood. Mrs. Henderson had sent them out to play in the garden and she could hear them laughing. Beanie, Robin and Danny came running to her directly she called, but it was several minutes before Mark, looking somewhat breathless and dishevelled, joined them.

'What have you been doing? Didn't you hear me calling you?' Fran asked with unwonted sharpness. Something about Mark's expression ... a hint of self-satisfaction ... made her feel faintly uneasy. He seemed to have forgotten all about this morning's upset, and that was unlike Mark, who often bore a grudge for days.

Mark's eyes were guileless. 'Sorry, Fran. I was looking for my ball.'

Fran frowned. 'Round by the greenhouses? I've asked you not to play ball there, Mark. Sam wouldn't be very pleased if there were any breakages.'

'I won't do it again.' Mark skipped past her and Fran frowned again. Excessive meekness wasn't one of Mark's characteristics either.

It was not until the next day that she discovered that her misgivings had been fully justified.

'Himself is back.' Mrs. Henderson greeted her with this information the moment she and the children walked into the kitchen for breakfast, and Fran's heart sank. No news could have been more unwelcome.

'I didn't hear the car.'

'I'm not surprised. It was after one when he got in.' Mrs. Henderson began cutting slices of thickly-buttered, golden-brown toast into 'soldiers'. 'I reckon as how he's used to burning the candle at both ends. He's been up since six: made his own breakfast. *And* washed up after himself and left the kitchen tidy.' There was no mistaking the note of surprised approval in her voice.

'There's Sam!' Beanie said suddenly, pointing towards the kitchen window. 'I say! Doesn't he look cross?'

'Like a thunder cloud!' Danny said in awe.

Fran looked up. Sure enough the old gardener was stumping rapidly towards the house, and even at a distance it wasn't hard to tell that he was in a towering rage about something. As he passed the kitchen window he paused for a moment, scowling horribly, and Fran felt that for two pins he would have shaken his fist.

She turned startled eyes on the housekeeper. 'Goodness! I wonder what on earth's upset him?'

'A plague of caterpillars, mebbe,' Mrs. Henderson said placidly. She was used to Sam's tantrums. She bent over Mark, who was the only one who hadn't finished his porridge. 'Come on, ducks! Eat up or you won't be ready for a nice boiled egg.'

Mark laid down his spoon. He had gone rather pale. 'I—I don't think I want an egg this morning. I'm not very hungry.'

Fran looked at him anxiously. Was he sickening for something? He'd been very quiet, almost subdued, ever since he got up. Perhaps he was fretting over those kittens after all.

'Well, I never!' said Mrs. Henderson. 'Fancy not wanting a nice new-laid egg!' She beamed round at the other children, who were all staring at Mark. 'They're the ones you brought me from the farm yesterday.'

'We collected them ourselves!' Danny's eyes sparkled at the memory. 'They were still warm!'

Fran laughed. 'Mr. Davis is very good to you, isn't he?' The children had spent many happy hours on his farm, earning themselves red cheeks and bright eyes ... not to mention grubby knees and hands, since good honest dirt was virtually inseparable from farms and animals!

'Can we go and see him today?' Usually it was Mark who asked this question: today it was Robin.

Before Fran could answer the kitchen door was flung open and Richard Quayle stood in the doorway, his hard eyes raking the room.

When he spoke it was with a steely inflection in his voice that Fran had heard before. 'I'm sorry to interrupt your meal, Miss Norton, but I shall be glad if you will spare me a moment.' It was very definitely an order and not a request, and the grimness of his face startled her. What on earth was wrong now?

She rose to her feet. 'I've finished.' With a quick word to the children she followed Richard Quayle out of the big sunny kitchen, her head held high. She was determined not to let herself be intimidated. In the hall Sam was waiting, and at the sight of him Fran's eyes widened.

'I'd like to show you something.' Richard Quayle forestalled the question that trembled on her lips. 'Come with us, please.'

Her heart beating suddenly faster, Fran followed the two men out of the house. Neither of them spoke, but that they were both furiously angry she was only too well aware. With a thrill of apprehension she realised that they were heading for the greenhouses. Mark ... and his ball! Had he broken a pane of glass? But if so, why all the dramatics?

It was not until they reached the second greenhouse that Richard Quayle opened his mouth again.

'Look inside, Miss Norton.'

Fran looked, and could not keep back the horrified exclamation that immediately rose to her lips. The greenhouse was a shambles. Shattered pots, earth and tangled, broken plants lay in wild confusion on the floor and on the shelves. It looked as though a tornado had swept through it.

Sam's voice was a croak. 'My prize plants! Ruined! All my work—wasted! If I could get hold of that young varmint——'

'That will do, Sam.' Richard Quayle cut him short. He turned to Fran, who was still staring at the debris with incredulous, horrified eyes.

'I don't suppose I need tell you, Miss Norton, that rightly or wrongly Sam believes that one of your children is responsible for this disgraceful act of vandalism. Have you anything to say?'

Fran licked her dry lips. She wanted to say that it was impossible, that none of the children would have done such a thing, but in her heart she already knew the name of the culprit. Mark! This was how he had avenged the kittens!

'Your silence seems to speak for itself.' Richard Quayle spoke in a tight, hard voice. 'I shall be glad if you will take immediate steps to find out who did this and bring him—or her—to me. I shall be in the library until eleven.'

He turned on his heel and walked away. Sam stooped down and picked up one of the broken plants with gnarled fingers that trembled a little.

'Why?' he muttered, shaking his grizzled head. 'Why?' He seemed to have forgotten that he was not alone, and Fran, who had started forward, her hand impulsively outstretched, let it fall to her side. The old man would not thank her for pity.

White-faced, sick to the bottom of her stomach, she walked slowly back to the house. How to deal with Mark she did not at the moment know, but about one thing she was determined. When she went to the library to report to Richard Quayle she would go alone, and whatever he had to say he could say to her.

Mark was in her charge, and this was her responsibility.

As she had anticipated, there was no difficulty in persuading the child to confess. Waiting for his crime to be discovered had completely unnerved him and he cried bitterly.

'He killed the kittens and made Matilda unhappy. I wanted to hurt him back,' he said between sobs. 'Fran, is Mr. Quayle very angry? Will we have to go away now?'

He was certainly a penitent sinner, Fran thought ruefully, but how much ice would that cut with a man as tough as Richard Quayle? Suppose he tried to insist on really drastic punishment? She shivered involuntarily, dreading the interview that lay ahead. Oh, he had a right to be angry ... she didn't deny that. Mark had done an enormous amount of damage ... some of it irretrievable. But there'd been a reason for his action, and Richard Quayle wouldn't understand that reason if he lived for a hundred years!

Later, in the library, he listened coldly to Fran's quiet statement that the culprit had confessed.

'Well, where is he? Too much of a coward to face the music?'

The contempt in Richard Quayle's voice made Fran's eyes blaze. 'The culprit, Mr. Quayle, is only six years old. I appreciate that it is your property that has been damaged, but the children are in my charge and are answerable to me and not to you.' Even if you *are* the master of Brocade. The words hung unspoken in the air.

Richard Quayle leaned back in his chair. 'And just what do you propose to do, Miss Norton? Punish him ... or award him a medal?'

Her eyes held his steadily. 'I find that remark offensive!'

'I beg your pardon.' He spoke ironically. 'I thought it was rather the thing these days for do-gooders to sympathise with the sinner rather than the sinned against.'

Fran flushed, recognising that he was being deliberately provocative. 'Mark *will* be punished. As far as I'm concerned, I can only say that I'm most desperately sorry about what has happened. I—I know that nothing can make up to Sam for the loss of those plants, but—but I would like you to know that I'm fully prepared to meet all the expenses.'

He stood up. 'Out of your own pocket?'

'Of course. The children are my responsibility. I stand *in loco parentis*.'

'And as I've told you before, you're much too young to have proper control over them.' Richard Quayle almost hurled the words at her. 'If I had realised that anything like this was going to happen I'd never have given permission for you to remain at Brocade! I assumed, wrongly it seems, that your charges were reasonably behaved children and not a pack of little hooligans!' He gave a bitter laugh. 'Tell me, am I to congratulate myself on my good fortune in not finding my pictures slashed, the walls defaced and bits chipped out of the furniture? Or am I not lawful prey? Is it safer to pick on a frail old man?'

Fran was white to the lips. Forgotten now were all her good resolutions to keep her temper at whatever cost.

'How *dare* you talk like that?' she said with passion. 'What do you know about children like Mark? You've always lived in a nice safe comfortable home, with people to love and look after you! Some people might say that you'd not turned out so marvellously even with all those advantages! What would you have been like if you'd been ill-treated, abandoned, homeless, unloved?' She paused for breath. 'At least Mark can love as well as hate! Do you know why he wrecked that greenhouse? Oh, it wasn't just for the hell of it, if that's what you're thinking! He did it because Sam drowned seven little kittens ... seven little kittens that Mark loved and was trying to protect!' To her horror she found her voice trembling and the angry tears welling up in her eyes. Dashing them away with the back of her hand she said passionately, 'Mark's only a child. To him, what he did seemed at the time to be just and right. Don't talk to me about hooliganism! There's more hope for Mark than there is for you! You aren't even human...'

She broke off, choking. She felt two steel-like hands grip her shoulders and Richard Quayle's low angry voice said, 'Be quiet! I didn't know about those kittens ... why didn't you tell me?'

She struggled violently for self-control. 'What difference would it have made? If you don't care about children, I don't suppose the fate of a few wretched kittens worries you overmuch!'

She broke off. 'I'd better go. I've said too much already. You've got a good excuse to get rid of us now. But I don't care ... I don't care...'

'Be quiet!' he broke in savagely. 'You little idiot! Listen to me for a moment!'

Just for a second he felt her quivering beneath his hands, then with a sob she wrenched herself free and ran out of the room, leaving the man staring blankly after her.

CHAPTER FIVE

IF anyone had asked her Fran would have said, when she went to bed that night, that nothing could possibly make her feel more depressed than she already was. When she woke up the next morning, however, it was raining hard and she groaned aloud as she saw the leaden skies. She knew she couldn't really complain—they'd been inordinately lucky to have had so much sunshine—but just at the moment the change in the weather seemed the last straw. The one thing she had counted on was being able to keep the children out of doors most of the day.

Fortunately, indoor games were something of a novelty and with the aid of a few jigsaws, a box of paints and one or two packets of marbles Fran was able to keep all five children reasonably happy and occupied until lunchtime. At intervals during the morning, however, she found herself wondering dismally when Richard Quayle would tell them to go. She was expecting a peremptory summons at any minute: she did not think it likely that he would either forgive or forget her outburst. The only thing that surprised her was that he had not already taken action. Perhaps, she thought ruefully, he was enjoying the feeling that he was keeping her in suspense.

Mark was still very subdued, so much so that Fran, despite the assurance she had given to Richard Quayle, had not the heart to punish him. Some time, perhaps, he would be willing to tell Sam he was sorry, but just at the moment Fran felt it was wiser to keep him and the old gardener as far apart as possible.

'Sam'll get over it. Just give him a few days,' Mrs. Henderson had counselled. She knew, of course, all about Mark's escapade and was somewhat shocked, though she admitted that he had had provocation. About Fran's subsequent interview with Richard Quayle she knew very little. (Despite her inner turmoil Fran had managed to regain her composure before returning to the kitchen, though possibly the housekeeper, noting her tear-bright eyes and flushed cheeks, had drawn her own conclusions.)

After lunch the rain, which had fallen steadily all morning, stopped, and a watery sun broke through the clouds. Immediately the children clamoured to go out and Mrs. Henderson asked Fran if they would like to walk down to the village.

'I want some oddments from the grocer's and I'd rather not go myself, I've got a rheumatic knee and it plays me up something cruel in wet weather,' she explained. 'Best put your raincoats on, though. It might not be fine for long: the sky still looks full of rain.'

She helped Fran to dress the children in mackintoshes and rubber boots, laughing at the picture they made for in every case the mackintosh was a little too large and they all wore floppy hats pulled down well over their foreheads. Fran herself came in for an approving look. She was wearing a new scarlet raincoat and the vivid colour suited her, enhancing her fairness and bringing out the iris-like delicacy of her skin.

'My, you're a sight to brighten up the dullest day!' Mrs. Henderson told her.

Fran laughed, her troubles momentarily forgotten. She and the children made a cheery little group as they splashed and sploshed their way to the village, careless of the dripping trees and revelling in the appearance of a rainbow and a large patch of blue sky. The narrow country road was full of ruts and holes, and pools of rainwater brimmed them all. To the children they were an irresistible invitation and they zig-zagged from one to another, shouting with glee and jumping in the middle of each one so that fountains of water shot up into the air.

Fran sniffed ecstatically. She loved the smell of earth and grass and flowers after rain, and she loved the freshness of the wind as it blew against her face. She was almost sorry when they reached the village, which was merely a cluster of thatched cottages, a fairly broad main street, a lovely village cross and one or two small shops.

The children begged for sweets and Fran bought them jelly babies and humbugs from the little post office before making her way to the grocer's. This shop was crowded and she had to wait some time before she was served. On her way out she almost collided with a slender, dark girl who was carrying a large shopping basket and who smiled pleasantly in acknowledgement of Fran's murmured apology, showing beautiful white teeth.

Something about her tugged at Fran's attention, but before she could indulge in idle conjecture Sue tugged at her arm and gave a gleeful shout.

'Look! There's the nice man who made my ear better!'

Sure enough Dr. Coates' somewhat battered convertible was parked just in front of the shop and the doctor himself was sitting behind the driving wheel, filling his pipe. He looked up at Sue's shout and, when he saw who it was, smiled and leant out of the window to greet them.

'Hello! How's the ear?' he asked.

'Much better, thank you,' Fran answered, since Sue, momentarily overcome by bashfulness, had retreated behind the boys.

Shyness was never likely to worry Danny. He was fascinated by the doctor's pipe, which was most intricately carved, and could not resist asking where it had come from. Told that it had been made by an

Australian aborigine, Danny's eager questions simply tumbled out and it transpired that Dr. Coates had at one time been part of the Flying Doctor service. That, of course, meant everyone crowding round and asking questions, and since Dr. Coates did not seem to mind answering them Fran did not attempt to interfere. She was listening as interestedly as the rest when a clear, sweet voice spoke from behind her.

'Enjoying your audience, Michael?'

It was the pretty dark girl Fran had seen entering the shop, but now she was not smiling. Her remark was addressed to the doctor, and with a faint shock of surprise Fran realised that she must be his wife, Rosemary. She was not in the least as she had imagined her. She was neither ultra-smart nor sophisticated: she was innocent of make-up and she wore her long dark hair in a simple, almost schoolgirlish style. But it was the wistful, haunting quality which hovered over her pale, heart-shaped face which puzzled Fran most. She was not, she thought suddenly, a happy woman.

Michael's face had lit up at the sight of his wife.

'I'd like you to meet Miss Norton, Rosemary. You remember I told you about her the other day?'

'I remember.' With perfect civility but not a great deal of warmth Rosemary Coates held out her hand. 'How d'you do?'

'How do you do?' Fran responded, and added laughingly, in order to carry off the situation, 'I suppose I ought to introduce each member of my family to you in turn, but I'm afraid there are rather too many names for you to digest all at once!'

'Yes, you have got a lot, haven't you?' Rosemary looked at the five children as she spoke and something in her voice—an almost passionate note of envy—caught at Fran's heart.

Oh no, she thought in dismay, not someone who can't have children of her own! There was an awkward little pause, then Michael Coates said, with an attempt at heartiness, 'If you're free on Thursday week, Miss Norton, could you come and have dinner with us? I've no surgery that evening and we haven't any other engagements, have we, Rosemary?'

'No,' said Rosemary in the same cool, polite voice she had used before. 'Do come.'

She sounded so unenthusiastic that Fran felt practically compelled to make an excuse, then she saw the almost pleading expression on Michael Coates' face and changed her mind.

'I'd love to,' she said warmly.

'Good. I'll come and pick you up about seven, if that will suit you?—Oh yes!' as Fran demurred. 'We live at the other end of the village, it's too far for you to walk from Brocade.'

Rosemary Coates made as if to get into the car, but before she could do so Beanie touched her arm. The little girl had been staring at her for several minutes and now she held out a bunch of wild flowers that she had plucked from the hedgerows on the way to the village.

'For you,' she said shyly, and smiled. Few people could resist Beanie's smile. She had a dimple in one cheek and none in the other, which gave her an appealingly comical, lop-sided look, and a missing tooth didn't help.

An odd expression crossed Rosemary's face. She hesitated for a moment, then 'Thank you,' she said gently, and took the straggly little bunch from the outstretched hand.

'I liked her,' Beanie confided as they walked home. 'She aminds me of my mummy.' Her voice was a little sad. Neither she nor Danny referred often to their mother. They had learned to accept her absence from their lives and Fran could only suspect at what cost.

Danny said, 'I like the doctor best. Do you think I could be a doctor when I grow up, Fran? A Flying

66

Doctor?'

'I don't see why not, if you work hard,' Fran told him. She felt a raindrop on her cheek and glanced anxiously at the sky. There were no longer any blue patches and the sun had disappeared behind the clouds. 'Right now, though, I think we'd better fly home. We don't want to get caught in another storm, do we?'

They all joined hands and began to walk quickly, but had not covered more than a hundred yards or so before it began to rain again in real earnest.

'Bother!' thought Fran. 'We're going to get soaked!' and picking Sue up in her arms she urged the others to run. As she did so a big car slid to a halt beside them with a hush of wet tyres.

The door was pushed open from inside and Richard Quayle's voice said, 'Get in. I'll give you a lift back to Brocade.'

Despite the rain Fran hesitated and even the children, who normally jumped at the chance of a ride in a car, hung back. Richard Quayle looked at them, at the children in their ill-fitting mackintoshes and absurd hats and then at Fran, who was bare-headed. The raindrops sparkled on her shining hair: its loosened rings curled around her neck and forehead.

An odd expression flitted across his face, then he said impatiently, 'For heaven's sake, would you rather be drowned? I'm not going to eat you, you know!'

Fran, still holding Sue in her arms, got in beside him without a word and Danny, Robin, Beanie and Mark crowded into the back. The car moved off.

Acutely embarrassed, yesterday's stormy scene still uppermost in her mind, Fran sat rigid. Richard Quayle's hands were square and capable on the driving wheel and he was frowning at the road ahead, his eyes narrowed against the driving rain. He did not speak and Fran, her mind a blank, could think of no way of breaking the paralysing silence.

In the end it was left to Danny. Heaving a huge sigh of satisfaction, he remarked to no one in particular, 'Isn't this a *super* car! I bet it's as good as James Bond's, except that I don't s'pose it fires bullets.' His voice was tinged with such regret that incredibly Richard Quayle's lips curved into a grim smile.

'You're quite right. It doesn't.'

'Oh well,' said Danny consolingly, 'you can't have everything. It's a smashing car all the same.'

'Thank you,' said Richard politely, and this time there was no doubt that the shake in his voice was a laugh.

Mercifully Danny relapsed into silence and the rest of the journey passed without incident. When they reached Brocade he brought the big car to a halt outside the front door of the house and leant over to open the back door for the children to get out. Sue scrambled off Fran's lap and there was a chorus of 'Thank you's.'

'Quick! Run in before you get wet!' Fran told them. She turned stiffly towards the man, wishing that his brown face were not quite so expressionless. Just at this moment she would give a good deal to know exactly what he was thinking. Well, if he intended giving them marching orders here was his chance!

'Thank you for the lift.' Rather to her dismay she realised that her voice sounded chillier than she had intended.

'That's all right.' His foot was already on the clutch: he was not, Fran thought with astonishment, going to say anything about yesterday after all. She turned to go, but before she had taken more than two paces he had called her back.

'Miss Norton!'

'Yes?' Fran's heart missed a beat. Was he playing some kind of cat and mouse game?

'You might like to know,' Richard Quayle said softly, 'that I have given instructions that no more kittens are to be drowned while I am the master of Brocade.'

He let in the clutch before she could answer and the car shot past her in a flurry of wet gravel.

Mrs. Henderson seemed delighted that Fran had been invited out to dinner and willingly agreed to look after the children for the evening.

'You don't have half enough time to yourself,' she said. 'It isn't natural, a pretty young girl like you being cooped up with a batch of youngsters all the time. You ought to go out a lot more often than you do.' She paused. '*And* with a nice young man.'

Fran said nothing. For a moment the older woman hesitated, her eyes on the downbent head, then she said gently, 'I know I'm a nosey old woman. But isn't there anyone, miss?'

Fran looked up, meeting the kindly inquisitive gaze steadily. Fair was fair, after all. She knew everything that there was to be known about Mrs. Henderson.

She said, 'There was—once,'

'And?' the housekeeper prompted.

'We were going to be married. A month before the wedding he wrote to me and told me that he'd fallen in love with somebody else. A girl called Julie.' Fran was rather surprised that she could speak so impersonally, almost as though what she was talking about had happened to somebody else.

Mrs. Henderson drew a long breath. 'Well, of all the dirty tricks...!'

Fran shook her head. 'Not really. I'm glad he was honest enough to tell me the truth. After all, what else is an engagement but a testing time? I'm only sorry he took so long to find out how he really felt, that's all.'

'Did he marry the other girl?'

'Oh, I expect so.' Fran made answer lightly. 'We lost touch: I don't really know what happened afterwards.' She rose to her feet. 'I'll make the cocoa tonight, shall I?' She didn't mind satisfying the house-keeper's curiosity, but the bare bones would have to suffice. There was something oddly distasteful about the dissection of an *affaire* long dead.

'No, I will.' Mrs. Henderson took the hint, as Fran had hoped she would, and did not probe further. To divert her thoughts into other channels Fran asked about Dr. Coates and his wife.

'Didn't you say they hadn't been here long? He was telling the children that he'd spent several years in Australia.'

Mrs. Henderson pursed her lips. 'They came about six month ago, I should say. Not longer. Dr. Coates took over when old Dr. Johnson retired.'

'He's made a terrific hit with Danny,' Fran said, smiling. 'He even got a special mention in his prayers tonight.' Since Danny's petitions to the Almighty were as brief as Fran would allow, that in itself was something of an accolade.

Mrs. Henderson nodded. 'I said he'd got a way with children. Pity he's got none of his own yet, isn't it?'

Fran was silent, remembering the way in which the children had clustered round the doctor this after-noon, like bees round a honeypot. She remembered, too, the expression in Rosemary's velvety brown eyes ... and wondered.

Mrs. Henderson put a steaming cup of cocoa in front of her. Fran would have preferred coffee, but cocoa was Mrs. Henderson's favourite bed-time drink and she made it hot and strong and sweet.

'It was nice of Mr. Quayle to give you a lift home this afternoon, wasn't it?'

She must have heard about that from the children, Fran thought. Aloud she said, 'Yes, it was.'

Mrs. Henderson sighed, her expression vaguely troubled. 'I've got a feeling he isn't going to stay here, you know. I thought he might be going to, all the trouble he was taking, but he told Sam this morning

70

that he means to go back to South Africa next month. Seems as though he's just going to put everything in order and then sell out.'

There was an anxious note in her voice which Fran could well understand. The chances were that if and when Brocade were sold she would lose her job as housekeeper.

She said comfortingly, 'Oh, I don't know. Brocade has been in the family for a long time, after all. Mrs. Eliot didn't seem to think he'd sell.'

The housekeeper sighed again. 'A house this size isn't much use to anyone unless they're going to live in it, is it? I'd like to know what he's got in mind, I'd feel a lot easier if I did!'

As it happened, Fran was soon in a position to tell her. The blustery weather continued, though it was mercifully dry, and the children spent a whole morning with sticks, newspaper, paints and string, making kites to fly in the home meadow. They were, of course, very crude affairs and Robin especially had difficulty in getting his off the ground. Eventually he brought it over to Fran who, her collar turned up, the wind whipping her hair this way and that, had perched herself on the top of a gate to watch them.

'Fran, why won't mine fly? It's no good at all!' he said aggrievedly.

Fran bent her head to examine it. 'Heavens, Robin, I don't know anything at all about kites!' She looked at it dubiously. 'Is it the right shape?'

'I think so. It's the same shape as Danny's and look how high his has gone!' Robin said, pointing.

A voice from behind them made them both jump. 'What about making your tail longer?'

It was Richard Quayle. Informally dressed in slacks and a crew-necked sweater, he had approached them unobserved and now stood with his hands in his pockets and the wind ruffling his dark hair. There was a quizzical gleam in his grey eyes, and Fran, conscious of the fact that her pose was hardly dignified, slid hurriedly to the ground.

Richard Quayle's lips quirked, then he held out his hand for the kite. 'May I see?—Yes, it's definitely your tail that's at fault. It needs to be a lot longer. What did you run out of? Patience or string?'

Robin looked sheepish and rubbed his right foot up and down his left leg. Richard Quayle laughed, delving into his pockets.

'I believe I've got an odd piece of string and some old envelopes. I'll help you to lengthen it.'

He squatted down beside Robin on the grass. Fran, looking down at the two heads, one dark and one fair, bent earnestly over the offending kite, felt almost like rubbing her eyes. She would never have believed that their unfriendly, unapproachable host was capable of unbending so far.

'There, try it now!' After a few minutes the man rose to his feet, watching critically as Robin, overjoyed, raced across the meadow, the kite billowing out behind him.

He turned suddenly to Fran. 'How did that child get that appalling scar?'

Fran told him.

'Good God! In this day and age?' Richard Quayle sounded revolted.

'The march of progress has nothing to do with wilful cruelty to children,' Fran told him dryly. 'In many so-called "primitive" countries the things that allegedly civilised people do to their offspring are quite unheard-of.'

Her eyes were on Robin's kite. Now the proud possessor of a long, long tail, it dipped and then soared high into the air. Robin shrieked with excitement and Fran laughed.

'That's *much* better! Thank you for coming to the rescue! I hadn't a clue what was wrong.'

'I used to fly kites in this meadow when I was

Robin's age.' Richard Quayle leant his elbows on the gate. His eyes were on the laughing children and the relaxation of the hard lines of his face made him look much younger. 'I believe I used to pray for windy days.'

Fran tossed back her unruly hair, her antagonism towards this man momentarily forgotten. 'I expect these infants will do the same, after this.'

'Excellent. Kite flying is a relatively harmless pastime,' Richard Quayle said dryly, and Fran flushed. She read into his apparently innocuous words a hidden meaning and was annoyed with herself for having been lulled into lowering her guard.

She could not think of a suitable riposte and remained silent, acutely conscious of the flicker of amusement in the hard grey eyes. After a moment or two he laughed.

'You have a very expressive face, Miss Norton. I can tell just what you are thinking.'

Fran's eyes sparked. 'Indeed? Then you must realise only too well that thought-reading, unlike kite-flying, is a relatively dangerous pastime, Mr. Quayle.'

He threw up one hand. 'Touché!' His eyes still mocked her. 'You're a very forthright young woman, aren't you? It's a refreshing change. My previous experience of do-gooders merely confirmed me in my belief that as a species they are as mealy-mouthed as they are tedious.'

'Will you *please* stop calling me a "do-gooder"? I didn't choose this job because of an obscure feeling that it might ennoble me! I just happen to enjoy working with children. Do you find that so very hard to understand?' Fran faced him indignantly, stung by the sheer injustice of what he had said.

'I'm afraid I do. But then I'm not even human, am I?' he asked sardonically.

So that had got under his skin! Fran drew a deep breath, but before she could answer Danny came running towards them, bulging cheeks scarlet with exertion, eyes sparkling.

'We're going to have a competition, to see whose kite goes the highest. Will you be the judge, please, Fran? You too, if you like, Mr. Quayle,' he added with scrupulous politeness.

Richard Quayle glanced at his watch. Incredibly he sounded regretful as he said, 'I haven't time, I'm afraid, Danny. I've got an appointment.'

'Who with?' Danny asked with interest.

'A builder.' He turned to Fran, the mocking protagonist giving way to the courteous host. 'These old houses present something of a problem, don't they? Chandeliers and open fireplaces might have been all right for my ancestors, but I must say I prefer something a little more up-to-date.'

Fran's face must have given her away again, for he gave her a sudden penetrating look.

'You don't agree?'

Fran flushed. 'I'm hardly in a position to agree or disagree. I just happen to think that Brocade is perfect as it is. You're very lucky to own such a beautiful home.'

The sincerity in her voice was unmistakable. For a moment the man was silent, then he said coolly, 'Beautiful, yes. A practical proposition, no. Houses like Brocade are only possible if they pay for their upkeep.'

'So you're going to sell?'

The dark brows lifted. Then 'Not at all,' said Richard Quayle gently. 'I'm thinking of turning it into a luxury hotel. I feel it should do very well, don't you?'

CHAPTER SIX

'A *hotel*? *Brocade*?' Mrs. Henderson's reaction to Fran's news could not have been more shocked if Fran had told her that Richard Quayle intended to turn his ancestral home into a house of ill-repute.

'That's what he said.' Fran spoke grimly. 'I couldn't believe it, either, but he definitely meant it.'

There was a pregnant pause, then the housekeeper sat down heavily in a convenient chair. 'Well, if it's really true it's a crying shame, that's what it is! Enough to make poor Sir Antony turn in his grave! A place like this swarming with trippers—oh, it just doesn't bear thinking about!'

Fran laughed a little shakily. 'Not trippers, Mrs. Henderson. Mr. Quayle very carefully stressed that it would be a "luxury" hotel! I expect he'll go all out to attract rich American tourists. It's the kind of place that will appeal to them, of course—they seem to like anything with a Past.'

Mrs. Henderson sniffed derisively. 'But *why*? What's he doing it for?'

Fran hesitated, torn between her own regret at Richard Quayle's proposal and a reluctant sense of justice.

'It's a question of economics, I suppose. It takes a lot of money to keep up a house the size of Brocade. Mrs. Henderson. It nearly beggared Sir Antony, Mrs. Eliot said, and even then, at the end, it became too much for him. You must have realised that yourself. Well ... Richard Quayle is a business man, first and foremost. He doesn't want Brocade for his home, but in order to keep it in the family, so to speak, he means to make it pay for itself.'

'He'd far better sell it!' Mrs. Henderson said bitterly.

'You couldn't be sure that the new owner wouldn't have similar ideas. People don't want large houses these days. But like you, I'm sorry. I'm glad I won't be here to see the chromium-plated bathrooms and the gilded cocktail bars,' Fran said sombrely.

She and Mrs. Henderson found that they were not alone in their feelings. Margot Eliot, tearing up to the house in her small red Mini, declared that she had every intention of telling her cousin exactly what she thought of his outrageous proposal. Thwarted by the fact that he had gone out for the day, she promptly unburdened herself to Fran.

'Isn't it *ghastly*? Oh, I know it's happened to lots of other stately homes, but there's no *earthly* excuse for Richard, he's simply rolling in money and he could keep up half a dozen Brocades if he wanted to!' she said bitterly. 'I've only just heard what he means to do—and then not from him but from the family lawyer! It—it's vandalism, that's what it is! I'd absolutely no *idea* that he'd got anything like that in mind!'

She looked tragically at Fran. Normally she would not have dreamed of unburdening herself to someone she knew so slightly, but she and Fran had been *en rapport* from their first meeting and the latter had always had the knack of inspiring confidences.

Frank knitted her brows. 'I wonder what made him think of it?'

'Oh, my dear, it's that wretched girl who's put him up to it! That's as plain as the nose on your face!' Margot said scornfully.

'What girl?'

'Oh, I forgot you wouldn't know!' Margot ran her fingers through her dark hair and laughed somewhat apologetically. 'How I do run on! But—well, I know you understand just how I feel, because of what you said to me about Brocade when I was here last. And I *can't* help feeling wild, because I'm certain sure that if it weren't for Suzanne Pleydell the idea would never have entered Richard's head! It couldn't have!'

'Who is Suzanne Pleydell?' Rather to her surprised annoyance, Fran found that she had to make a conscious effort to make the question sound completely casual.

'A girl Richard knows in South Africa. Her father owns a huge chain of hotels and she works for him in Public Relations or something. Apparently she's very astute: Richard and she are well suited, I'd guess!' Margot stubbed out her cigarette with unnecessary violence. 'I don't really know a great deal about her, actually, but those friends I was telling you about—the ones who live in Johannesburg—say that she and Richard are frightfully thick. And apparently, according to Joan and Peter, she's coming over to England in a week or two, to give poor old Brocade the once-over. And as she already seems to think that it's got commercial possibilities—well, I can only suppose that it will end up a joint venture!'

'Oh!' said Fran. She could think of nothing else to say, though inwardly she was devoured by curiosity. 'She and Richard are frightfully thick...' Just what did Margot mean by that? And what was Suzanne Pleydell like? She must be someone rather special, if she appealed to a man as hard-bitten as Richard Quayle appeared to be.

Margot's next question took her completely by surprise. 'What do *you* think of him? Richard, I mean?'

'I—well, I—that is, we haven't seen much of him,' Fran floundered. She was furious to find herself blushing.

Margot sighed. She had half hoped that her maddening cousin might find himself attracted to Fran. She really was a honey. But Richard, of course, was

77

almost bound to conduct his love life as he seemed to conduct everything else—with cold-blooded precision. He would probably make sure that if and when he married there would be considerable 'fringe benefits' ... and Suzanne Pleydell, though described by her Johannesburg friends as spoilt and selfish, happened to be the only daughter of an immensely wealthy man.

After Margot's visit Fran found herself speculating about Suzanne Pleydell, her relationship with Richard Quayle and the ultimate fate of Brocade rather more frequently than she liked. None of it had anything at all to do with her, she told herself severely, and made up her mind to discipline her wayward thoughts. After all, there was little point in speculation anyway, since long before Suzanne Pleydell made an appearance at Brocade she and the children would be back in London.

Or so she thought, until another letter from Miss Challoner made her realise that she was being over-optimistic. Apparently the necessary repairs and renovations to No. 17 were proceeding very slowly and it now seemed more than likely that it would be the end of the summer before the house would again be fit for habitation.

'I have been in contact with Mr. Quayle and he assures me that you and the children are quite welcome to stay at Brocade until such time as No. 17 is ready for you,' Miss Challoner wrote. 'So you see there's absolutely nothing to worry about. Mr. Quayle really sounds quite charming: he couldn't possibly have written me a kinder or more considerate letter...'

Fran had writhed inwardly at that last remark. She was quite sure that Richard Quayle's tongue had been very firmly in his cheek when he had written that 'kind' and 'considerate' letter to Miss Challoner. He must be simply longing to get rid of them, and in all honesty, who could blame him? Not that they saw much of him: at the moment he seemed to be spending most of his time in London.

There was no sign as yet of any of the drastic alterations to which he had referred—presumably, Fran thought wryly, he was waiting for Suzanne Pleydell's verdict!—but builders were busy repairing the roof, which apparently leaked badly in several places, and restoring some of the ancient stonework. Mrs. Henderson was engaged in a positive orgy of cleaning and though she now had two women from the village to help her, had very little spare time. Fran missed her cheerful companionship, for much as she loved the children and fascinating though she found them, she sometimes felt a little cut off and isolated. In London, there'd always been friends dropping in at No. 17.

As the day approached, she found herself looking forward with mixed feelings to her engagement to dine with Michael and Rosemary Coates. She liked the former very much, but was slightly unsure about Rosemary. She would have to know her a little better before she could make up her mind.

Michael came to fetch her, as he had promised, and drove her to a big, rambling old house with an extremely pretty garden.

'Rosemary loves gardening. It doesn't matter how many cobwebs flourish in dark corners as long as weeds don't show their faces in her flower beds!' Michael said laughingly as he led Fran up to the front door.

Rosemary met them in the hall and to Fran's surprise and relief her manner was much more friendly than it had been on the occasion of their previous meeting. It was obvious, too, that she had taken extra pains with her appearance and she was looking very pretty, in a slim-fitting, gold-coloured dress that suited her. Only her eyes belied the gaiety of her smile. There was something in their dark depths that Fran did not even begin to understand.

The meal was excellent—shrimp cocktail, roast duck and then an exotic creamy concoction of Rosemary's own invention—and the three were soon chatting away like old friends. Possibly Michael and Fran did most of the talking, but nevertheless Rosemary made a delightful and animated hostess. Fran found it hard to believe that she was unable to make friends easily—not, at least, if she was usually like this. But which was the real Rosemary? Was her present gaiety merely a mask? If so, she was careful not to let it slip, and the evening was well on the way to being a resounding success when the telephone rang.

'Damn!' Michael put down his coffee cup and rose to his feet. 'I hoped that cursed instrument would have the decency not to ring tonight!' He excused himself and went out into the hall, reappearing a few moments later looking rather grim.

'Sorry, folks. I'm afraid you'll have to do without me for half an hour or so. It's an urgent call.'

'Somebody having a baby?' Rosemary asked, and at the sound of her tight, brittle voice Fran glanced at her in surprise. Surely she had been married to a G.P. long enough to have become used to this kind of thing?

'No, it's not a baby,' Michael answered her shortly, and turned to Fran. 'I'll try to be as quick as I can, and anyway I'll be back long before you need to go home.'

'Oh, please don't worry about me!' Fran exclaimed, and looked ruefully at Rosemary as he went out. 'I suppose we must be thankful that at least he's had his dinner!'

Rosemary shrugged. To Fran's dismay there was a distinct downward droop to her wide sweet mouth. 'A G.P. leads a dog's life. He's at everyone's beck and call—except mine, of course.' She laughed without amusement.

There was a tiny silence. Then Fran said quietly, 'You must be very proud of him. He's a splendid doctor, isn't he? He was so good with Sue when she had earache: the children all adore him.'

She realised immediately that she had said the wrong thing. The mask had not only slipped, it hung painfully awry. 'Oh, yes!' Rosemary said bitterly. 'He always did think a lot of *other* people's children!'

She looked at Fran with eyes that were suddenly almost black with misery. 'I suppose you've been wondering why we haven't any family? Sooner or later everyone wonders the same thing. They think it's my fault that we haven't. Well, it isn't.'

Fran sat in acute discomfort, at a loss what to say.

Rosemary clasped her hands round her knees, the simple, childlike gesture oddly at variance with the bitter resentment she now made no attempt to hide.

'I'm going to tell you what happened. I don't bother, usually, people can think what they like and I just don't care. You're different, somehow.' She spoke in strained tones, her eyes on Fran's face.

'Rosemary ... look, there's no need——'

'I was going to have a baby.' Rosemary ignored the interruption and her words fairly tumbled out. 'We were so pleased, Michael and I ... a child was what we both wanted more than anything else in the world. Those nine months we waited for it to be born were the happiest of our whole marriage. We planned all the time for the baby ... we thought about nothing else, at least I didn't, and Michael was nearly as bad. He helped plan the nursery ... he kept bringing home absurd toys ... and he booked me in at the most expensive nursing home he could find, miles away from our home.' She stopped, her face drawn with remembered pain. 'It was going to be a spring baby. When the pains began it was a lovely sunny day and the garden looked wonderful. I remember thinking as

I got into the car that when we came home the lilac would be out to greet us ... and that if I was going to park the pram anywhere near the kitchen window I'd have to cut back the honeysuckle.' She stopped again, running her tongue round her lips. 'We were half-way to the nursing home when just as he rounded a bend a child toddled out into the road straight in front of us. We hadn't a chance. There isn't a driver in a million who'd have been able to avoid hitting him, but Michael ... Michael swerved just in time. We skidded across the road and hit the bank on the opposite side. I don't remember anything else, except that when I recovered consciousness they told me my baby was dead. And that I could never have another.'

Fran leant forward and caught hold of her hand in an agony of compassion. 'Oh, Rosemary, I'm so sorry!'

'That's just what Michael said, over and over again. But it made no difference. Our baby was dead.' Rosemary spoke with such dreary hopelessness that Fran almost winced.

'Rosemary—it was a dreadfully cruel thing to happen. But Michael had to swerve: he had no choice. And you wouldn't have wanted him to have acted any differently.'

Rosemary shook her head. 'No. But that doesn't stop it hurting.'

'I suppose you couldn't—have you thought of adoption?' Fran asked the question hesitantly, but was unprepared for Rosemary's swift, almost violent reaction.

'No! A thousand times no! That's what Michael wants, but I'll never agree! I couldn't bear it, Fran. I couldn't let some other child take my baby's place.'

Fran was silent. There were so many things she could have said, but she knew that Michael would have already said them all.

After a moment Rosemary said in a low, tense voice, 'Yes, I know that you're happy, looking after other

82

people's children. But you don't have to, do you? And you're lucky ... you'll be able to have your own one day.'

Fran looked straight at her. 'That's rather in the lap of the gods, isn't it? But one thing I *can* tell you, Rosemary, and that is that I don't think I could love Mark and Danny and Beanie and the others very much more if they really were my own. And I'm quite sure I don't need to tell you how well adoption works out for most people, or how much joy and comfort they and their chosen children bring to each other.'

Rosemary sighed. 'Maybe. All the same, I can't bring myself to do it. I don't even like children as much as I used to.' She looked wistfully at Fran. 'So don't think I'm completely horrid if I don't make much of a fuss of yours, will you?'

'Of course not. I understand how you feel.'

'Good.' Rosemary jumped to her feet and it seemed to Fran that she was already regretting her burst of confidence. Certainly she had once again reverted to her role of bright, smiling hostess.

'More coffee? This is cold. I'll make some more.'

When she had gone Fran looked around her and sighed. The white-panelled, many-windowed sitting room was attractively furnished, but for comfort rather than for elegance. It was really rather a hotch-potch of old and new, yet somehow all blended together to create a most pleasant impression. Rosemary seemed a born homemaker ... was probably a born mother. There should be tenderness in her face, not sadness. If only she could put her tragedy behind her ... eradicate the bitterness that was poisoning her life ... and fill up the empty spaces in her house and in her heart!

For the rest of the evening Rosemary chatted gaily on a number of inconsequential subjects and Fran, following her lead, was careful not to make the slightest reference to children. She was glad, however, when Michael came home, and guessed from the slightly anxious expression on his face as he looked from her to his wife that he was wondering what had transpired during his absence.

Her guess was confirmed when in the car, going home, he asked hesitantly whether Rosemary had accepted an invitation to Brocade.

'I felt it was kinder not to extend one.' Fran thought it best to be frank.

'Oh.' There was a short pause, then she added quietly, 'I know how she feels, you see. She told me about the baby.'

'She did?' Michael sounded frankly incredulous, but quickly recovered himself. 'I'm—glad. It means she must like you. I thought she would.'

'I like her, too. And I'm very sorry for her,' Fran said gravely. 'She's extremely unhappy, isn't she?'

'Unhappy?' Michael gave a short mirthless laugh. 'She's changed completely in the last year. The baby ... I know it was a terrible blow, but I thought—I hoped—in time she'd get over it. I've done every mortal thing I can, but it's no use. She just won't put it out of her mind. If only she'd agree to adoption...' He gave a despairing shrug.

'Perhaps later on...?'

'Perhaps.' Michael's voice showed that he did not hold out much hope. He turned the car into the drive leading to Brocade and stopped outside the front door. The house was in darkness, but the moon was shining. As Fran made to get out he detained her. Reaching over into the back of the car, he produced a miscellany of bulky objects.

'I wondered if the children would like these?' he asked, somewhat awkwardly. 'I happened to be passing a toy shop in Cheltenham today and—well, I bought a cricket bat for each of the boys and a doll for the two girls. Nothing very exciting, but...'

'Oh!' Her arms full of the packages, Fran gazed at

him in delight. 'They'll be absolutely *thrilled*! How very kind of you to think of them!'

'Not at all.' Michael's smile was cheery. 'Tell the boys I'll try to find time to come and have a game with them one evening.'

'They'd love that,' Fran said warmly. Although she did her best to be both father and mother, she was sometimes painfully aware that the children missed a masculine influence in their lives. The boys especially. (She had discovered to her secret amazement that even though he had made no secret of his dislike for them they all looked up to and admired Richard Quayle immensely.)

She watched the car disappear down the drive, then turned to walk round to the back of the house. She had never used the front door of Brocade since the advent of its owner.

'Ten minutes past midnight. Time all civilised people were abed.'

Too late she saw the faint glow of a pipe and realised that Richard Quayle was standing in the shadows. The unexpected sound of his deep, familiar voice made her jump and—merely because she was startled, of course—she found her heart beating unaccountably fast.

'Oh!' she said foolishly. 'I didn't know anyone was there!' In her confusion she dropped one of the bats: she bent to retrieve it, only to find that Richard had forestalled her. For one moment their cheeks were almost touching and she heard the sudden swift intake of his breath before they both stood up.

'Thank you.' She took the bat, and he said brusquely, 'I'm sorry if I startled you. I saw the car coming, but I didn't realise you were in it.' He glanced up at the sky. 'Nice night, isn't it?'

'Perfect.' She wished desperately that her heart would stop thudding against her ribs.

'I'm glad you found someone to share it with.' The

moon had momentarily disappeared behind a cloud and so she could not read his expression, but she was acutely aware of the familiar note of mockery in his voice. Mockery—and something else that she did not even try to analyse.

She said coldly, 'I don't quite know what you mean by that, but I've spent the evening with Dr. and Mrs. Coates. It was Dr. Coates who brought me home. And now, if you'll excuse me, I must go in. Mrs. Henderson may be waiting up for me.'

'Don't use the back entrance!' He spoke peremptorily and as she turned to look at him in blank surprise he added roughly, 'You don't look like a kitchenmaid. Why behave as though you are one?'

Too taken aback to answer, she followed him silently up the steps and through the big front door into the hall. He switched on the light.

'Goodnight, Miss Norton.'

'Goodnight.' She crossed the hall quickly, conscious of his eyes following her. His attitude astonished and confused her, but she was far more upset by her own reactions. The mere sight of that wretched man was beginning to be enough to put her off her balance!

Mrs. Henderson had not gone to bed. When Fran entered the kitchen she was sitting at the big, well-scrubbed table. A writing pad was in front of her and she was chewing the end of a ball-point pen.

She shook her head and laughed at Fran's reproachful greeting.

'You're not still working, Mrs. Henderson? Look at the time! It's past midnight!'

'I wanted to get this letter written. I've been thinking about it most of the day, but I don't seem able to get it right,' she said, and sighed as she screwed up another piece of paper to join the crumpled balls on the floor beside her. Then she turned a carefully-smiling face to Fran's. 'Well, had a nice evening?'

'Lovely, thanks.' Fran deposited her parcels on a

chair in order to take off her coat, and Mrs. Henderson's brows raised.

'Been shopping, have you?'

Fran laughed, glad to find herself recovering her usual equilibrium. 'Gifts from Dr. Coates for the children. Won't they be pleased?' She withdrew one of the bats from its wrapping and held it up for approval.

Mrs. Henderson pursed her lips. 'Maybe. But Sam won't if they use those cricket bats on his precious lawns!' she said dryly.

'Don't worry! Cricket will be strictly prohibited except in the home meadow!' Fran retorted. She bent to pick up the crumpled pieces of paper, amused to find that in moments of stress Mrs. Henderson's usual orderliness deserted her.

'Income Tax trouble?' she asked, laughing.

'No, I'm writing to Johnny.' Mrs. Henderson sighed again. 'He's gone and got himself engaged. He told me when he was here that he was thinking of popping the question, but I begged him to take his time. He's only known the girl a few weeks: it isn't long enough, to my way of thinking. I only hope she's a nice lassie and not some flibberty-gibbet!'

'I'm sure you can rely on Johnny's good taste! Anyway, I expect you'll meet her soon,' Fran said consolingly.

'That's just what I won't do. No sooner had Johnny bought the ring than she upped and left him! Seems her father is ill and she's gone back to Dublin to look after him and help her mother.' She pushed the writing pad away. 'I don't think I'll write tonight, after all: maybe I'll know better what to say when I've slept on it. Come and have a cup of cocoa before you go to bed, miss, it's all ready.'

'Have the children been good?'

'Lambs! I haven't heard a peep out of them!' Mrs. Henderson told her. She glanced across at the parcels.

'I suppose you'll give them their presents directly they wake up? They'll be off their heads with excitement: reckon there'll be no need for me to set my alarm!'

Mrs. Henderson's prophecy proved correct. The children were enchanted with their gifts and Fran, watching their rapturous faces as they inspected their new treasures, stored up their excited comments to retail to Michael.

'Look, my dolly's got curly hair!' Beanie said proudly. Her own straight locks were a continual source of grievance: she longed for soft natural ringlets like Sue's.

'Mine's got real shoes that take off!' Sue rejoiced.

'Huh! Dolls!' Danny said scornfully. 'Who wants *dolls?* Look at my bat, Beanie! Isn't it a beauty?' He stroked the bat with loving fingers. He'd always wanted a cricket bat and now he'd got his wish.

From somewhere downstairs he heard the sound of a door being opened and shut. That must be Mrs. Henderson. He'd go and show her his bat: she'd be sure to admire it!

He jumped off the bed and was half-way down the stairs before Fran realised he had gone.

'Danny! Come back! You're not dressed!' she called.

Danny did not check his headlong flight and heaving an exasperated sigh, Fran flung on her dressing gown. The little monkey knew quite well he wasn't allowed to bother Mrs. Henderson before breakfast!

The housekeeper was not in the kitchen. Disappointed, Danny was about to return upstairs when, as he crossed the hall, he caught a glimpse of her dusting the ornaments in the drawing room. This was forbidden territory as far as the children were concerned, but in his excitement Danny forgot that.

He rushed into the room, gleefully brandishing his bat.

'Look, Mrs. Henderson! Look what I've got! A

cricket bat! I'm going to hit the ball for *miles*! Look! Like this!' He struck up an exaggerated pose and before the startled housekeeper had divined his intention had swung the bat back and up. As he did so the edge of the bat hit a Sèvres vase standing on a small gate-legged table and there was an ominous crash, followed by an appalled silence.

CHAPTER SEVEN

'OH, Danny! How *could* you!' Fran stood in the doorway, her face whitening as she realised what had happened. Danny, the bat still in his hands and looking the picture of guilt, was staring blankly at the fragments of porcelain on the floor. For once in her life Mrs. Henderson's ready tongue had failed her: she was speechless with dismay.

Fran knelt down on the floor and, picking up one of the fragments, held it in the palm of her hand. She knew at once what had been broken: she had admired the beautiful vase many times.

'It was a n'accident.' Danny's voice was small and scared. Child though he was, he knew from the expression on the grown-ups' faces that this was far more serious than a broken cup or saucer.

With a visible effort Mrs. Henderson pulled herself together. 'Don't be too cross with him, miss. He was too excited, that was his trouble.' In spite of herself her face crumpled, for she had always prided herself on the way in which she had cared for the objets d'art Sir Antony had prized so much. 'But I don't know what Mr. Richard will say to me, and that's a fact.'

Fran rose wearily to her feet. 'You won't have to tell him, Mrs. Henderson. That's my job.'

It would be she who would have to bear the brunt of his anger, and at the thought of the unpleasant scene that doubtless lay ahead even her courageous spirit quailed. She hadn't forgotten the last time yet. This was different ... Danny hadn't *meant* to break the vase ... but Richard Quayle wasn't the sort of person to make allowances for accidents. He was almost bound to be simply furious.

She turned to Danny, trying to keep her voice calm but not succeeding very well. 'Go and get dressed, Danny. And please be careful what you do with your bat in future. You've done quite enough damage as it is.'

'It was a *n'accident*!' Danny repeated desperately. He couldn't understand it. He knew he shouldn't have gone into the drawing room, but usually if something got broken and it was an accident, Fran understood and she didn't get cross. Why was it different this time?

'An expensive accident, ducks,' Mrs. Henderson said grimly, stooping to help Fran pick up the rest of the fragments.

Danny swallowed. 'Did—did it cost a lot?' His heart sank as Mrs. Henderson nodded.

A hundred pounds at least, Fran thought, though it could be even more, she really knew very little about the value of old porcelain. Oh, if only it were possible to replace it! If only she didn't have to face Richard Quayle and tell him what had happened! What was it he had said ... that other time? 'Am I to congratulate myself on my good fortune in not finding my pictures slashed, the walls defaced and bits chipped out of the furniture?' Well, he wouldn't congratulate himself any longer!

All through breakfast dread of the ordeal ahead kept her unusually silent and she ate very little. It wasn't the end of the world, it was silly to behave as if it were, but she couldn't help it. Somehow she didn't seem capable of rational behaviour where Richard Quayle was concerned!

Danny guessed the reason for her grave face and squirmed unhappily. Fran was worried about telling Mr. Quayle that his vase was broken. It wasn't fair, he thought suddenly, that she'd got to do it. It wasn't her fault, so why should she take the blame? She'd told him a hundred times that he mustn't bother Mrs.

Henderson before breakfast, only he'd been so excited that he'd forgotten.

He drew a deep breath. He didn't really blame Fran for being afraid of Mr. Quayle. He did look a bit scarey sometimes. But not always. When he smiled his eyes crinkled up at the corners and he looked quite different. Perhaps, Danny thought hopefully, if he owned up about the vase he wouldn't be so terribly cross? And even if he was ... well, at least he'd be cross with the right person. Fran needn't know anything at all about it until afterwards.

He made up his mind. Directly after breakfast he'd go and find Mr. Quayle and tell him what had happened. The prospect made his stomach feel a bit fluttery, but that didn't matter, except that like Fran he didn't feel much like eating.

He gazed hard at his plate. The only thing was, he ought to offer to pay for the vase, and that was a bit awkward because he'd only got twopence-halfpenny and probably the vase had cost a lot more than that. Maybe ten shillings, or perhaps even a pound, though that wasn't very likely. Who'd be silly enough to pay a whole pound for a vase? But whatever it had cost it made no difference. He hadn't a hope of getting any more pocket money before Saturday, and even then it would only be sixpence.

A sudden inspiration struck him. He could offer to give Mr. Quayle something in exchange for the vase— something that really *was* valuable. His cricket bat must have cost an awful lot of money, it was such a nice one. His small fingers clenched convulsively. Oh, he couldn't part with it! He simply couldn't! And what would Dr. Coates say if he did? For a moment the magnitude of his contemplated sacrifice over- whelmed him, then he swallowed hard. It would just have to be the cricket bat. He hadn't got anything else.

His chance came after breakfast, while Fran was

helping with the washing up. He went out into the garden with the others, but as soon as he could do so unobserved he slipped away. Beanie was the only one who knew where he was going. He had had to tell her, in case she noticed that he was missing and made a great fuss. She'd wanted to come with him, but he wasn't having any of that! Mr. Quayle *would* think he was a cissy!

Clutching his precious bat in hands that were suddenly damp and sticky, he crept to the library. He knew Mr. Quayle was in there, he'd seen him through the window, sitting at his desk. By the time he'd reached the door he was almost shaking with fright, but his courage did not fail him. He knocked and waited.

'Come in.' Richard Quayle looked up from his desk as the door opened, expecting to see Mrs. Henderson. Instead he saw a pale-faced little boy whose dark eyes were brimmed up with a mixture of desperate courage and shrinking terror.

For a moment Richard Quayle did not speak, then he leant back in his chair. Danny saw to his immeasurable relief that even though he wasn't smiling his eyes were crinkling at the corners. At least he wasn't cross—yet.

'Good morning, Danny. To what do I owe the honour of this visit?'

Danny hadn't the slightest idea what he meant, but the amused interest in his voice gave him courage. He went forward, holding out the bat and speaking at express speed, his words tumbling over each other in his haste to get them out.

'Please, I've come to tell you that I'm very sorry I broke your vase. I didn't mean to, it was a n'accident, and you're not to be cross with Fran 'cos it wasn't her fault. And I'm very sorry, I can't pay for it 'cos I've only got twopence-ha'penny and Mrs. Henderson says it cost a lot, but you can have my bat instead. I s'pect it's worth much more than the vase 'cos it's brand new, I only had it this morning, but it will have to be that 'cos I haven't got anything else to give you.'

Richard Quayle looked at him steadily, something in his eyes which might have been the beginning of a twinkle. 'Do you mind saying all that again, a bit more slowly this time? I—I'm afraid I haven't quite grasped it.'

Danny looked at him despairingly. 'Do you really want me to say it *all* again?'

'If you please,' Richard said courteously.

Danny took a deep breath and standing with his feet planted well apart, his hands clasped behind his back, he repeated his explanation more slowly and with rather more detail.

In the meantime Fran had discovered his absence. This was simply because poor Beanie, unable to stand the strain any longer, had dissolved into copious tears. She was sure that the terrifying Mr. Quayle would be so cross about the broken vase that he would do something quite terrible to her beloved brother.

'Danny? Gone to see Mr. Quayle?' Fran stared at her incredulously. 'Beanie, he hasn't?'

'Yes, he has,' Beanie sobbed. 'And he's been gone *ages*!'

Fran wasted no more time on words. Richard Quayle—and Danny! She did not quite know what she expected to find, but when she reached the library and heard the rise and fall of voices she did not wait to knock but catapulted herself through the open door like a wildcat defending her young. Then she stood stockstill in sheer surprise. Richard was sitting at his desk and Danny was perched on the arm of his chair, laughing at something he'd said and looking very much at home.

Richard looked up and saw her, amusement gleaming in his eyes as he read her expression aright.

'Ah, Miss Norton! I've been wondering when you'd

94

make an appearance!'

'Danny——?'

'Is perfectly safe with me. I'm really not the sadistic monster you suppose me, you know. I don't go in for torturing small boys—even when one of them *has* broken a piece of my priceless porcelain!'

'Then you know——?'

'Indeed I do.' Richard's eyes held dancing devils. 'Danny came, very properly, to tell me what had happened and to make an *amende honorable*. He's offered me his cricket bat as compensation.'

'But he won't take it.' Danny grinned at Richard, making no secret of his immense relief. 'He's just going to borrow it whenever he feels like playing cricket. We've got an—an understanding.' He brought out the word triumphantly.

'Oh!' Fran said blankly. She looked helplessly from one to the other. She could hardly believe that there'd been no need for all her heartburning, but she had the evidence of her own eyes and ears. Richard Quayle was as unconcerned about his piece of priceless porcelain as if it had been a half-crown vase from a jumble sale.

'You can cut along now, Danny.' Richard smiled at the child, then turned to Fran, his smile deepening. 'Don't look so worried, Miss Norton. Danny took considerable pains to assure me that this morning's little contretemps was not your fault.'

Fran drew a deep breath and faced him squarely, her eyes full of honest distress.

'But it was. Danny was careless, but then so was I. It's my job to see that—accidents—of that nature don't occur. It's my responsibility, and so I must apologise too.'

His eyes mocked her. 'Then tell me, do you think that Danny has offered me adequate compensation?'

Fran flushed. 'If you will let me know what the vase was worth——'

He rose to his feet, and as always she found his face inscrutable. 'Never mind its monetary value. Shall we say, Miss Norton, that I shall feel myself more than compensated if—to match Danny's princely gesture—you will do me the honour of dining with me this evening?' He smiled down into her astonished face, enjoying (she thought) her discomfiture and taking her silence for consent. 'I'll expect you at seven-thirty. Don't be late.'

He held the door open for her as he spoke and Fran, almost dumbfounded, made good her escape.

It was with reluctance bordering on trepidation that Fran dressed for dinner that night. As she looked at her reflection in her mirror, pinching her pale cheeks in order to bring some colour into them, she felt as though she would have given almost anything for a last-minute reprieve. She couldn't imagine why Richard had extended the invitation: it couldn't possibly be that he liked her or found pleasure in her company, so what was his motive? Puzzled, suspicious, she was very much on the defensive, so much so that watching her as she sipped her sherry Richard suddenly broke into a low laugh which held an underlying note of irritation.

'My dear girl, do relax! I have no Borgia-like inclinations and I can assure you that this excellent sherry is neither drugged nor poisoned!'

Frank looked straight at him, her colour rising. 'Will you please tell me why you wanted me to dine with you tonight? I'd like to know.'

For a moment he looked taken aback, then, surprisingly, he grinned.

'You *do* favour the direct approach, don't you? Perhaps you've caught that from young Danny. I've noticed that he doesn't go in much for circumlocution!'

'You haven't answered my question.'

He looked down at his glass so that she could not see his eyes and his voice was non-committal.

'I merely thought that it was time we had a friendly chat and got to know each other a little better. You see, I rather gather that you and the children are going to be my guests for quite a while longer.'

Fran's fingernails dug into her palms. 'I know. I'm sorry. I only wish there was something I could do about it: we've trespassed on your hospitality long enough.'

He said quietly, 'I don't want you to feel like that. I know I was unwelcoming at first, but that was because I was—unprepared. I meant what I said when I told your Miss Challoner that I was happy for you to stay here for as long as you wished.'

Feeling as though she was in some wild, improbable dream, Fran gave a shaky laugh. This Richard was far more disquieting than the old one had been! With an attempt at lightness she said, 'I could almost suppose that you'd changed you mind about disliking children!'

He laughed too, rising to his feet as Mrs. Henderson announced that dinner was ready.

'You may be surprised to know that I am beginning to discover that they have their occasional virtues as well as their manifest failings!' he said, and this time the warmth of his smile left her feeling oddly shaken and breathless.

She reflected on her way into the dining room that nice or nasty, the less she saw of Richard Quayle the better it would be for her peace of mind!

Throughout dinner he was a relaxed and pleasant host, but though Fran forced herself to reply to his easy conversation she was still a little on her guard, and it came as a shock when she suddenly realised that she was enjoying herself immensely. Possibly, she thought, her surroundings had something to do with it. The huge panelled dining room was candlelit and the soft light seemed to enhance the glowing harmonies of the wonderful old refectory table ... polished walnut wood, pale, bright silver and sparkling glasses.

Fran, sitting opposite Richard, accepted wine merely for the pleasure of drinking it out of one of the beautiful crystal goblets which she knew were family heirlooms. She held the glass in her hand, admiring the tracings of vines and leaves in gold, and it seemed to the man, watching her, that her hair, like a nimbus of spun gold around her head, sparkled and gathered to itself all the light there was.

'Aren't you ever bored here? Don't you sometimes long to get back to civilisation again?' The question seemed to come out of the blue.

Fran wrinkled her brow. 'I don't know that I agree with your concept of civilisation! But in answer to your question, no, I'm not. I was happy in London, but all the time I missed the country. Whenever I woke up in the morning and heard the roar of the traffic I used to feel an odd little pang of regret. Here, I lie and listen to the rustling of the leaves. At night they're like a lullaby. This is such a peaceful place ... it seems to have some sort of magic quality.'

There was a smile in the grey eyes. He quoted softly:

'And this our life, exempt from public haunt,
Finds tongues in trees, books in the running
*   brooks,*
Sermons in stones and good in everything.
I would not change it.'

His lips twitched at her surprised expression. 'What's the matter? Is it so incongruous that I should know my Shakespeare?'

'That particular bit, yes,' Fran said unguardedly, then coloured. 'I'm sorry. I suppose that was rather rude.'

To her relief he laughed outright. 'Not at all. I admire your candour. I think you might tell me, though, what Shakespearean passage you consider it would have been more appropriate for me to memorise?'

He was teasing her now. She laughed back at him, refusing to meet his challenge.

'I'm not really well up on Shakespeare.'

'I don't suppose you have much time to be well up in anything,' he said drily. He leant back in his chair and subjected her to a thoughtful scrutiny. 'I must say that being a housemother seems a queer job for a girl like you. What on earth made you take it up?'

Had he asked the same question earlier in the evening Fran would have hedged, but now, though she hesitated a little, she answered with her usual truthfulness.

'I suppose it was because I myself had such a blissful childhood. My father is the rector of a small country parish and I and my brothers and sisters were brought up in a huge old barn of a rectory. We—we had space and time in which to think and grow, parents who loved us and pets and books and pictures and friends. I—I suppose that as I grew up I began to realise how unfair it was that we had so much, when others had so little.'

She stopped, afraid even now of his possible derision, but though there was a wry twist to his lips his eyes held none of the mockery she had come to expect. What he would have said, she never knew, for just at that moment there was a gentle knock on the door.

'Would you like coffee in here or in the drawing room, Mr. Quayle?'

Mrs. Henderson did not look at Fran as she spoke, but Fran knew at once that there was something wrong. The housekeeper's face was strained and anxious and her voice sounded jerky.

She looked quickly at Richard. It was unlikely, she

thought, that he would notice anything amiss, but again he surprised her. Obviously he was very much more perceptive than she had thought.

'Is anything the matter, Mrs. Henderson?'

The housekeeper hesitated, obviously reluctant to allow a trouble of her own to burden other people, but the kindly concern in Richard's eyes seemed to decide her.

'It's—well, it's my son, Mr. Quayle. My youngest son, Johnny.' Her work-roughened fingers nervously plaited the edge of her apron. 'I've just had a phone call to say he collapsed in the street today and had to be taken to hospital.' She was obviously trying hard to sound matter-of-fact, but failed miserably: Johnny, to her, was still her baby, and she loved him dearly.

'Oh, I *am* sorry!' Fran and Richard spoke in unison.

'What's the matter with him? Nothing serious, I hope?' Fran enquired anxiously. She had liked cheerful Johnny.

'Overwork and nervous fatigue, the hospital say. Apparently he's been working all day and studying all night,' his mother said grimly. 'He always was one for burning the candle at both ends. I knew no good could come of it.'

'Of course not. You must let me know if there's anything I can do to help,' Richard said.

Fran leant forward. 'He'll be well looked after in hospital, Mrs. Henderson. But what about afterwards? He'll have to have a complete rest, and didn't you tell me he lived in rather unsatisfactory digs?'

There was a moment's silence. Richard looked at Fran, a gleam of amusement in his grey eyes, and then at his housekeeper.

'I'm afraid that aspect of the matter hadn't struck me. You'd better tell him to come to Brocade when he's discharged from hospital, Mrs. Henderson. Then you can keep an eye on him.'

Surprise, relief and gratitude struggled for expression on Mrs. Henderson's face.

'Oh, that *is* good of you, Mr. Quayle! I wouldn't have asked, but I'd feel a lot easier in my mind, if you're sure it'll be all right?'

'My dear Mrs. Henderson, I don't suppose Johnny's presence will make the slightest difference to me or to anyone else!' Richard said, laughing. 'Please make whatever arrangements you like.'

He waited until she had gone, still uttering fervent thanks, then looked at Fran and spoke with mock severity.

'I have an appalling fear that if I am continually exposed to your benign influence I shall become a do-gooder myself! What, do you think, possessed me to invite Johnny Henderson to partake of my hospitality? I assure you that I had not the slightest intention of doing so until I saw you eyeing me as hopefully as a dog eyes a bone!'

Fran's eyes were dancing. 'I'm sure your good deeds won't go unrewarded!'

'I wish I shared your certainty.' Richard rose to his feet. 'I think Mrs. Henderson has probably forgotten the coffee after all. Would it be too unkind to remind her?'

'I'll go and ask her,' Fran said quickly. 'And if you don't mind, Mr. Quayle, I think I ought to stay with her. It isn't very pleasant being alone when one is worried and anxious, is it?'

For a moment he said nothing, looking at her with penetrating eyes that seemed to see right into her mind. Then he said gently, 'No. It's not pleasant,' and there was a note in his voice she did not understand.

Later, after Mrs. Henderson had gone to bed, cheered and comforted, Fran moved softly about the little sitting room, putting things away, for though she never made a fetish of tidiness she had an innate love of order.

'May I come in?'

Preoccupied with her thoughts, Fran had not heard the sound of approaching footsteps, and it was with a shock of surprise that she saw Richard's broad frame silhouetted in the doorway.

'Yes, of course, please do!' She cast a wild look round her. Thank goodness she'd cleared away most of the children's scattered belongings and the room was reasonably tidy!

He held out a tiny, lace-edged handkerchief. 'I found this. Your property, I believe?'

'Yes, it is. Thank you.' Fran found herself blushing with confusion. Why had he brought it back tonight, instead of letting Mrs. Henderson find it in the morning?

'This is the first time I've been in this particular domain.' Richard was looking thoughtfully round the room. 'You're quite comfortable in here? There doesn't seem an awful lot of room for such a large family.'

'We manage beautifully,' Fran assured him.

He wandered over to the table and picked up a tiny dress and bonnet she had been making for Sue's doll.

'What on earth——?'

'Clothes for Sue's doll. She and Beanie are very fashion-conscious,' Fran explained with a laugh.

'And this?' He put the tiny garments down and picked up a cardboard model aeroplane in the last stages of construction.

'Danny asked me to help him with that. It's rather complicated for a small boy.'

Richard's brows raised. 'You do look after them a little beyond the line of duty, don't you?'

'I don't think so. You've forgotten how much little things like that mean to children,' Fran said steadily.

'Forgotten?' Richard gave a short laugh. 'It might be more accurate to say I never knew. For all their dependence on the Welfare State, I envy your children. They have each other, and they have you. They're luckier than I was.'

Fran stared at him, open-mouthed.

'B-but . . .' she stammered.

'The picture you drew some time ago of my favoured childhood was a little wide of the mark, I'm afraid.' Richard's voice had an edge to it. 'Oh, materially I was very well off, I grant you that. I was brought up in a delightfully clean, hygienic nursery completely isolated from the rest of the house. A most efficient and competent nurse was engaged to look after me, her chief duty being to ensure that I was absolutely no trouble to my parents. Like you, I grew up with— what were your words?—space and time in which to think and grow. Unlike you, I also grew up with the knowledge that nobody wanted me. Not surprising, perhaps—I was frequently left in no doubt that I was a most unprepossessing child.'

Fran's face had grown white. It was never really forgotten, what happened to you in childhood. Physical wounds healed, often without a scar left on the tender skin. But the other kind of hurts . . . they rarely disappeared without trace. And the scars they left still ached and throbbed.

She said childishly, conscious of its sheer inadequacy, 'I'm sorry.'

'And so am I. For wallowing in self-pity.' Richard was himself again, utterly assured, at ease. That moment of stark revelation might never have happened. Deliberately he changed the subject.

'I have a confession to make. I didn't seek you out tonight merely to return your handkerchief. I particularly wanted to ask you if you would be willing to do something for me.' He paused, and she had the impression that he was searching for the right words.

'I'm expecting a visitor in a few days' time—a friend from South Africa. She'll be staying here for a week or two and it's possible that I may not always be free to entertain her. As you probably know, I'm having to spend quite a lot of my time in London: this end of my firm's business has been rather badly neglected for several years and I'm having to pull things up a bit. If you'll be willing to befriend Suzanne I'll be more than grateful.'

'Yes, of course.' Fran hoped that her all-too-expressive face did not reveal the dismay she could not help feeling.

'You'll find that she's extremely keen on the idea of turning Brocade into a hotel: in fact, the suggestion originally came from her.' Richard's voice was carefully non-committal. 'I hope, knowing your views on the subject, that you won't find her enthusiasm for the project too upsetting?'

A smile lurked in his eyes as he said this, and Fran flushed.

'That would be rather silly of me, wouldn't it? I can assure you that I'll do all I can to help, Mr. Quayle.'

'I think you might start by dropping the "Mr."' This time Richard's rare smile lit up his whole face and Fran's heart did a crazy somersault. 'I've heard the children calling you "Fran". What is it short for? Frances or Francesca?'

'Francesca. My parents rather went in for grandiloquent names, I'm afraid. I've one sister called Cordelia and another Benedicta.' Fran strove to speak lightly.

'Fran!' said a small voice at that particular moment, and Sue, a diminutive figure in rose-sprigged pyjamas, weaved her way sleepily across the room, rubbing her eyes with her small chubby fists.

After one amazed moment Richard burst out laughing. 'Just *how* does one obtain an uninterrupted conversation with you?' he asked. 'Does this kind of thing go on all the time?'

Sue climbed on to Fran's lap and fixed Richard

with a bright, interested stare.

'What's he doing here, Fran?'

'I might ask you the same thing!' Fran said with mock severity. 'Why didn't you call me if you wanted me? Look, no slippers!' and she pointed to the bare pink toes.

'I fought I'd come down instead. Want a drink of water,' Sue explained.

She took several tiny sips from the glass Fran provided for her, then held up her arms with an angelic smile.

'Carry, please!'

Fran bent to pick her up, but Richard forestalled her.

'What, up all those stairs? My dear girl, you'll be dead! Here, young lady, let me be your chariot!' and he swung her easily up into his arms.

'Oh, no, please, I can manage perfectly!' Fran exclaimed, but Sue was crowing with delight and Richard was already making for the stairs.

'There! No more gadding about tonight, please, Your Highness!' he said, laughing as he deposited Sue in her small bed next to the sleeping Beanie's. Fran, utterly amazed, bent over her to tuck in the blankets, and Sue, determined to exploit the situation to the nth degree, spoke sleepily but imperiously.

'Sing me a song!'

'Certainly not!' Fran said hastily. 'I'll wake Beanie.'

'*Nothing* wakes Beanie.' (This was true, Fran thought ruefully.) She added reproachfully, 'You *always* sing me a song afore I goes to sleep, you know you do!'

That was true, too. Fran looked despairingly at Richard. If only he'd go! She simply couldn't sing to Sue with him standing at her elbow!

But Richard showed no sign of departing and Sue was becoming indignant.

'Go on,' the man said quietly, and after a moment's

hesitation Fran obeyed. She hadn't a strong voice, but it was low and pure and sweet.

> 'Bed is too small for my tired head,
> Give me a hill topp'd with dreams
> Tuck a cloud up under my chin,
> Lord, blow the moon out, please.
>
> Rock me to sleep in a cradle of dreams,
> Sing me a lullaby of leaves,
> Tuck a cloud up under my chin,
> Lord, blow the moon out, please.'

As she sang, Sue's lashes drooped over her pink cheeks. Fran's voice died away and she looked up and met Richard's eyes. He straightened abruptly, made as if to speak, changed his mind, and turning, went quietly out of the room.

CHAPTER EIGHT

RICHARD had told Mrs. Henderson that Johnny's
presence at Brocade wouldn't make the slightest
difference to anyone. Perhaps it didn't, to Richard,
who treated Johnny at all times with a casual good
humour, but Fran and the children soon found that
life had taken on a new flavour.

Protesting that he felt perfectly well and that
everyone was fussing unnecessarily over his health, he
firmly refused to be treated as an invalid. The only
concession he made to his mother was an undertaking
not to open any books, and he spent as much of his
time as possible out-of-doors.

He spent many hours helping Sam in the garden—
there was always so much to do that any extra
assistance, even unskilled, was a boon to the old
man—but he also saw a good deal of Fran and the
children. He had quickly lost his initial shyness with
Fran and they were soon on the friendliest of banter-
ing terms. Mrs. Henderson, listening to the ceaseless
badinage that went on between them, occasionally felt
sorry that Johnny had already lost his heart to his
Irish colleen. She would have loved Fran for a daughter-in-law, though she was honest enough to admit to
herself that even if there were no Eiluned Fran was
unlikely to have considered Johnny as a possible
husband. He was too young, for one thing—only two
months older than Fran—and at times, quite unconsciously, she treated him almost like one of the children. He asked for it, of course, his mother thought:
he could be just as daft as Mark and Danny and
Robin when the mood took him. And though Fran
was amused and interested, she would require some-

one very much more mature as a life partner.

Fran, of course, knew all about Eiluned. Sure of a sympathetic audience, Johnny talked about her for hours, so that in the end Fran felt she knew her almost as well as he did.

'You needn't have the slightest misgivings,' she told Mrs. Henderson. 'She sounds a thoroughly nice girl. I like the way she's thrown up everything—flat, job, Johnny—to go home to look after her parents in a crisis. Devotion like that is worth quite something these days. Johnny is a lucky man.'

Although she often assured herself that it was Johnny's companionship which had suddenly made life at Brocade so much more pleasant, Fran knew in her heart of hearts that it wasn't the sole factor. It was amazing how much Richard's change of attitude had affected her. She felt so much more relaxed and confident now that she was no longer living in daily fear of herself and the children being blown up sky high.

She never really knew quite how it came about, but somehow or other she had formed the habit of dining with Richard each evening he was at home. In this way an odd kind of friendship developed between them and as she came to know him better she even began to understand him a little. She could see how the lonely, unhappy little boy, surrounded by every luxury and yet lacking the basic essentials of a normal, carefree childhood, had grown into a complex, reserved, self-sufficient man ... a man who knew what he wanted, who had the world taped and who drove himself mercilessly. Yet there was another side to him, and she sometimes found herself wondering a little forlornly which was the real Richard ... the ruthless, rather arrogant man prepared to ride roughshod over everyone or the man who could not bear to think of new-born kittens being drowned, who could win the confidence of a child and show sympathy and consideration towards his employees. A man of many parts ... that was Richard.

To the children their host remained something of an unknown quantity, for he was not often at home during the day. He still spent a great deal of time in London, so much so that Fran found it surprising that he did not stay in town altogether. Perhaps, she thought, after a gruelling day he was glad to escape to the peace and serenity of the country. There must be a welcome contrast between the hurly-burly, cut-throat life of a high-powered executive and the quiet tempo of life at Brocade, where it seemed as if all the richness, warmth and peace of past centuries had been retained and held secure.

Rather to her surprise, on Sunday he was at church, sitting alone in the family pew a little ahead of Fran and the children. After the service he was introduced by the Vicar to Michael and Rosemary, and Fran later heard from Rosemary that he and Michael, although so dissimilar, had taken to each other at once.

Perhaps the encounter put him in a good mood, for when later in the day he came across Fran, Johnny and the children playing cricket in the home meadow, he needed little persuasion to join in the game. He shared Danny's bat in accordance with their 'understanding' and was seemingly genuinely amused by the boys' enthusiastic if wildly inaccurate attempts at batting and bowling.

Fran, who was a novice at the game, was out first ball when it was her turn.

'Oh dear! No one else has suffered such an ignominous fate, not even Beanie!' she said, laughing as she surrendered her bat to Johnny.

Richard made no comment, but when it was her turn to bat again she found that he had taken it upon himself to issue detailed instructions.

'No, don't hold your bat that way!' he told her as

she took her stand before the wicket. 'Look, hold it like this.' He guided her hands to the right position on the handle of the bat, and as he did so she suddenly shivered, despite the warmth of the afternoon. Frantically she tried to concentrate. How hard and brown his fingers were! There was a signet ring on the little finger of his right hand ... she could see a crest engraved upon it. Another family heirloom?

Suddenly she realised that he had not relaxed the pressure of his hands and she glanced up, startled, to find him looking at her with an expression in his eyes which completely baffled her ... the same expression she'd noticed the night he'd carried Sue upstairs and she'd sung her to sleep. Confused, she felt the colour surge into her cheeks and her lashes flickered, then his hands dropped abruptly to his sides and he said, almost brusquely, 'Now try!'

This time she fared better, but she was glad when a delivery from Johnny eventually sent her middle stump flying. She preferred to be an onlooker and felt that she would always remember the timeless quality of the drowsy summer afternoon and retain in her mind a vivid impression of the scene now before her eyes. It was the kind of picture which might belong to any family album ... the two men, one tall and lithe, the other shorter but well-built, silhouetted against a backcloth which had not changed much since the days of Queen Elizabeth I, and laughing boyishly as they attempted to instruct the children in the rudiments of England's national game.

Fran enjoyed watching Richard because he moved so easily, with a lithe grace, but she had to admit that Johnny was actually very much the better cricketer. As a result of his prowess, coupled, of course, with the fact that he was nearly always available for games and expeditions, he was held in the highest esteem by the children. Then, a day or two later, something happened which put Richard way ahead in the popularity stakes and made Mark, at least, his devoted admirer for all time.

Fran had taken the children out for a picnic in the woods and they were returning home when Richard's sleek grey car overtook them in the drive. She was a little surprised to see him since she knew that Mrs. Henderson had not been expecting him back until late evening, but evidently nothing was wrong for when the children waved and smiled he waved back. Then, apparently as an afterthought, he wound down the window and called out to them, 'Hurry up! I've got something to show you!'

Immediately the older children were on the point of taking to their heels, but Fran, mindful of Sue's short legs and the fact that she would be unable to keep up with the rest, firmly checked their headlong flight. By the time they reached the house, therefore, Richard had had time to park his car and he was sitting waiting for them on the stone balustrade.

'What's he got?' Danny's voice was puzzled, for his sharp eyes had noticed that Richard appeared to be holding a small black bundle in his arms.

'It's alive!' Beanie shouted, for just at that moment the black bundle wriggled and squirmed its way out of Richard's arms. It landed in a sprawling ungainly heap on the grass, scrambled up on to its stubbly legs, caught sight of Fran and the children and gambolled towards them, waggling a wispy appendage which was presumably meant to be its tail.

'It's a *puppy*!' Mark's voice was almost a squeak as he rushed forward to fall on his knees beside the ridiculous little creature, which had now rolled over on to its back and was waving its podgy paws in mid-air. In a moment the other children had followed his example and were paying extravagant homage to the stranger in their midst; eyes shining, cheeks rosy with delight.

Richard strolled across the lawn to join them, hands

thrust deep into his pockets, amusement and—yes, satisfaction—showing plainly on his face.

He looked at Fran and laughed. 'What do you think of him?'

'He's sweet!' Fran, who loved all small, helpless things, spoke warmly. 'He's a Labrador, isn't he?'

Richard nodded assent and Mark lifted a radiant face.

'What's his name, please, Mr. Quayle?'

'He hasn't got one yet, I'm afraid. Any ideas?' Richard asked.

There was dead silence while everyone thought frantically. Then Beanie piped up in her shrill little treble.

'It's Monday today! You could call him Little Dog Monday, couldn't you?'

'Monday!' Richard repeated the name thoughtfully. 'Yes, Beanie, I like that. It's original. Monday it is.'

'He *is* yours, isn't he?' Robin asked anxiously, and for a moment tragedy lurked in everyone's eyes. They hadn't realised before that there was an awful possibility that Monday belonged to someone else, someone who didn't live at Brocade.

Richard put their minds at rest.

'Well,' he said, smiling slightly, 'he *is* mine, in a way, but I've got rather a problem. Puppies need a lot of looking after, and just at the moment I'm very busy. Do you think, until you have to go back to London, you could count him yours and look after him for me? Feed him and take him out for walks and so on?'

There was another long silence while every child savoured the glorious prospect. A dog of their own! A dog to love and train and talk to and play with! Oh, it was too good to be true! They'd never been able to have one before: London wasn't the place for dogs, Miss Challoner always told the housemothers.

Fran, watching their radiant faces, felt a lump come into her throat and she turned impulsively to Richard. Would she ever understand this complex man?

'Have you any idea how happy you've made them?'

Richard laughed. 'I certainly hoped he might appeal!'

'Does Mrs. Henderson know about him yet?'

'She does not,' Richard admitted ruefully. 'I bought him rather on the spur of the moment, I'm afraid. I saw some black Labrador puppies advertised in to-day's *Times* and drove out to see them at lunchtime. That little beggar'—and he nodded towards Monday—'more or less demanded to be chosen. He was the most playful of the bunch.'

Fran said quietly, 'I don't believe you really wanted a dog. It was more than good of you to think of giving pleasure to the children.'

For a moment he looked intently into her face. Then, 'Not only the children,' he said enigmatically, and turned away to offer a helping hand to Sue, who had been literally bowled over by Monday's friendly overtures. (Not, judging from her fat chuckles, that she minded a recumbent position in the least!)

Fran felt the colour creep up under her tan and she stood for a moment staring after Richard until a chuckle at her elbow made her jump. She had forgotten Johnny, who had been a silent but interested spectator.

'You know, I rather think mine host has a soft spot in his heart for you, girl dear! How d'you like the idea of being mistress of Brocade one day?'

Johnny's blue eyes were brimful of laughter. Fran's first impulse was to utter a vehement protest, but she thought better of it. Johnny would never let her hear the last of it if she rose to his bait. Of course he didn't really think there was any truth in what he'd said, he was merely being provocative, but for some reason or other she was hideously embarrassed.

She decided that in order to squash Johnny at the outset she would have to contrive to keep out of Richard's way until Suzanne arrived. Then the situation should be clear enough even to Johnny.

Unfortunately for her good resolutions, Michael rang up that evening to invite both her and Richard to dinner on the occasion of Rosemary's birthday. Richard accepted the invitation with alacrity and Fran felt that under the circumstances it was impossible for her to do anything but accept also. She had not seen as much of Rosemary as she would have liked: it was difficult, during the day, to do much visiting, and in the evenings she had been busy making some new cotton dresses for Beanie and Sue. (Dressmaking wasn't a task she enjoyed, but the little girls' pleasure in their new clothes made her feel that her efforts were well worthwhile.)

She had wondered a little about the success of a foursome made up of herself, Richard, Rosemary and Michael, but she need not have worried. It was a delightful evening. Richard was at his most charming, and produced a humorous side which Fran had never thought he possessed. They all did a good deal of laughing, even Rosemary, and Fran, watching Richard's grey eyes twinkle at her across the table, suddenly found herself realising anew that when he liked he could be most formidably attractive. She bit her lip. Thoughts like that were definitely to be discouraged! All the same, there was no denying that this gay, light-hearted Richard was a very different person from the brusque, stern autocrat who had caused their early days at Brocade to be so fraught with difficulties.

Rosemary was talking to Richard about his home.

'I can't tell you how much I admire Brocade,' she said in her clear, musical voice. 'I always feel that those great old houses are very much more than mere buildings—they're a part of England, part of the very fabric of our lives. It's good to know that there are still people like you willing to preserve tradition and beauty whatever the cost.'

Fran held her breath. Evidently, then, Richard's plans concerning Brocade were not yet public knowledge. She waited for him to announce his intention of turning the house into a hotel, but to her surprise he answered Rosemary briefly and immediately changed the subject.

Soon after midnight the party broke up. Naturally Fran went home with Richard, but though she started off by chatting gaily she quickly subsided. For some unknown reason Richard had suddenly lost his good spirits and was silent and preoccupied. She wondered why. It was such a wonderful night: the moon was riding high in a star-spangled sky and the air was balmy and sweet-scented.

When they reached Brocade they both, by unspoken consent, sat in silence for a few moments before saying goodnight. Fran had never been able to decide to her own satisfaction whether Brocade was more beautiful in moonlight than in sunshine, but tonight there was no doubt in her mind at all. Tonight the old house was a thing of dream and glamour and enchantment. The garden was full of mysterious dancing shadows and the spreading branches of the majestic trees were tipped with silver.

'Penny for them,' Richard said unexpectedly, and she turned to find him watching her thoughtfully.

She laughed a little shamefacedly, suddenly confused at having him so near, but she answered frankly.

'I was just wishing that there was some way of capturing time ... of making it stop at a given moment for ever and for ever.'

'How unadventurous!' he said teasingly. 'How do you know that there aren't some even better moments round the next corner?'

She laughed, glad that he seemed to have recaptured something of his earlier mood.

'I don't know, of course. But I don't believe that I'll ever see anything more beautiful than Brocade in the light of a full moon.'

'You love it, don't you?'

'Yes,' Fran said simply.

For a moment he did not speak. Then he said quietly, 'You know, some time before my uncle died he wrote to me and told me that he was leaving Brocade to me. He said that it hadn't been his real wish to leave it to someone who had made a country other than England his home, but that he had no choice, since if he left it to Margot it would be more of an encumbrance than a blessing. There was no money to go with it, you see.' He paused. 'He asked me for a definite assurance that I'd never sell it unless I was absolutely forced to. I gathered that it meant a tremendous lot to him: for years he'd scrimped and saved and sacrificed to keep Brocade looking beautiful, and his most passionate desire was that it would come to mean something to me, the only one left bearing his name.' He shrugged slightly. 'Needless to say, I was between the devil and the deep blue sea. I didn't want Brocade: I had a perfectly good home in Johannesburg and I'd severed all my English ties long ago. The whole thing was a bore ... an utter nuisance. But I promised. God knows why, but I promised.'

'And an old man died happy,' Fran said quietly. Remorse had seized her. How could she ever have thought Richard completely hard ... utterly ruthless?

'Yes. But then my problems began. What did one do with a house that one didn't want, but couldn't sell? Suzanne's ideas about the hotel ... it seemed, at the time, a heaven-sent compromise.'

'At the time...' What exactly did he mean by that? 'And now?' Fran prompted.

He did not answer her directly. Instead he got out of the car and stood for a moment with his back towards her, looking towards the house. Then he walked round to her side of the car and opened the door.

'Suzanne arrives the day after tomorrow. I heard from her this morning,' he said, and the unexpected harshness of his voice was like a blow in the face.

'Oh!' said Fran. There was nothing else to say, but she felt a cold hard knot form inside her stomach and wondered at the feeling of desolation which swept over her. It was ridiculous to feel like that about a girl she didn't even know ... a girl whom Richard had asked her to befriend!

In bed, some time later, she reproached herself bitterly: 'You're all sorts of a fool, Fran Norton. You're less than nothing to Richard Quayle, and the sooner he and his wretched house become nothing to you, the better. Stick to your job of looking after the children and making them happy—and let Richard and Suzanne work out their own problems, even if they turn Brocade upside-down and inside-out in the process!'

On the day that Suzanne was due to arrive Fran took the children out for a picnic. Mrs. Henderson packed them up enough food to feed a garrison, and they and Monday spent several blissful hours roaming in the woods and on the hills. Fran, knowing from experience what was likely to happen, made sure that everyone, including herself, was wearing old clothes. It was no good expecting children to enjoy themselves if they had to worry all the time about what they were wearing! Her precautions were justified, for at the end of the afternoon they were all looking sadly in need of a hot bath and clean clothes, so much so that Fran reflected ruefully that it was just as well that they didn't have to walk back through the village. They would be bound to meet just the one person who thought that dirt was synonymous with neglect!

She glanced at her watch. Mrs. Henderson had been told to expect Richard and his visitor any time after seven o'clock. It was now nearly five, so she would have plenty of time to get the children back to Brocade, bathed and in bed before Suzanne arrived.

She called everyone together and they set off for home, the children in high spirits and Fran trying valiantly to suppress the ridiculous qualms she was feeling about Suzanne's imminent arrival. They had almost reached the house, still laughing and chattering gaily, when Fran suddenly stopped dead in her tracks. An expression of incredulous dismay spread over her face. Richard was just emerging from the rose garden, not a hundred yards away! Richard ... and a slender, graceful girl in green ... Suzanne! Whatever were they doing here already? It was nowhere near seven o'clock! Panic-stricken for no reason that she could think of, she half-turned to tell the children to go back, but it was too late, they too had spotted Richard. With shrieks of joy they rushed towards him, Monday barking excitedly, and she saw Richard smile and say something to Suzanne as he bent to stroke the puppy. Then they both strolled forward to meet her and she became acutely conscious of Suzanne's critical gaze.

'Hello, Fran! I've just been telling Suzanne about you and the children,' he said smilingly.

Suzanne extended one white, languid, rose-tipped hand (so very different from hers! Fran thought ruefully). Very good-looking, with her glossy black hair and ivory skin, she was also strikingly elegant: in fact, she looked as though she might have stepped straight out of the pages of a fashion magazine. Her suit was superbly cut and of the loveliest shade of amber imaginable. The expensive silk scarf knotted carelessly round her white throat perfectly and exactly matched her lipstick, not a hair of her head was out of place, and every single thing about her pointed to an ideal marriage between money and impeccable taste.

Fran, whose own attitude to clothes was cheerfully

haphazard, suddenly became searingly aware of her own faded jeans and the shirt she'd bought from a chain store two years ago. Not only that, she wasn't wearing a vestige of make-up and her hair was tied back in a pony-tail. She flushed uncomfortably under Suzanne's supercilious stare, for she had no way of knowing that in actual fact the other girl was rapidly revising her automatic assumption that anyone who chose to look after other people's children must necessarily be fifty or a frump!

She said, with a cool, brittle smile: 'I've just been telling Richard how much I admire his philanthropy. It isn't everyone who'd have been *quite* so noble, is it?' Her amused, slightly scornful glance rested on the children, who, shy in the presence of a stranger, had drawn close to Fran.

Richard said sharply, 'Philanthropy my foot! I'm enjoying their stay.' If he hadn't smiled as he spoke it would have been a very definite snub, and as it was a peculiar expression crossed Suzanne's face, so fleeting that afterwards Fran was to wonder whether she'd imagined it.

'I don't like her,' she thought as she hurried the children round to the back of the house. 'And she certainly doesn't like us either!' For just before they were out of earshot she'd heard Suzanne say, still in that hateful amused voice, 'Darling, do they *always* look so dirty? Doesn't she ever bother to wash them or anything?' What Richard answered she did not know, but a second later she'd heard Suzanne's tinkling laugh and had writhed inwardly.

Johnny, predictably, was outspoken in his comments.

'Mine host can certainly pick 'em, can't he?' he said with a grin. 'Cleopatra and Helen of Troy rolled into one! Not that she's my type, all the same. Too many airs and graces for my liking!'

'Johnny, hold your tongue and mind your own

business!' Mrs. Henderson said, sharply for her. Not, judging from her expression, that she herself was altogether smitten with Richard's guest, and- Fran guessed that she would probably have plenty to say later on. Somehow she felt she could not bear to hear the matter spoken of in Mrs. Henderson's gossipy matter-of-fact way, and in order to avoid an unwelcome discussion she went out for a walk in the grounds after the children had gone to bed, driven by a restlessness she did not begin to understand. It was a lovely evening, warm and still, and there was a spectacular sunset which lit the sky with fire.

Instinctively she made for the home meadow, but as she neared the gate a murmur of voices made her stop and draw back with a sharp intake of her breath. Richard and Suzanne were standing together in the shelter of the hedge, staring out over the green grass at the distant hills, and the two dark heads were very close.

Immediately Fran moved back, intending to slip away unobserved, but a twig snapped beneath her foot and Richard turned and saw her.

'Hello. Too nice an evening to stay indoors, isn't it? You should have kept the children up a bit longer and we could have all had a game of cricket!'

There was no help for it. Trying to ignore Suzanne's annoyed expression—'I suppose she thinks I followed them on purpose!'—Fran moved forward to join them.

'I suppose you're admiring the view? This is a lovely spot, isn't it, Miss Pleydell?'

'I suppose so.' Suzanne shrugged her slender shoulders. 'Actually, though, I haven't really noticed the view. I've just been thinking that, properly converted, this would make a simply ideal car-park. What do you think, darling?'—turning to Richard. 'We'll need a big one, you know.'

The home meadow—a car park! Acres of tarmac

where there was now lush green grass starred with daisies: sleek shiny cars where there were now birds and tiny creatures; the sound of strident horns and running engines where there was now peace and serenity!

Fran blurted out in horror, 'Oh no! You *can't* do that!' then bit her lip and grew crimson. She looked guiltily at Richard and was relieved to see the understanding in his eyes before he shook his head in quick negation of Suzanne's proposal.

'No go, Suzanne. We'd never get planning permission, to start with. And even if we did—well, Fran is quite right. It *is* a lovely spot—too lovely to spoil.'

There was a look of furious incredulity in Suzanne's dark eyes. She had set her heart on turning Brocade into a hotel—it was just what she needed to bring her and Richard closer together. She had arrived at Brocade expecting to find him as enthusiastic about the project as he had been when she had first mooted it, and instead he had been infuriatingly non-committal. What had been going on these last few weeks? Had he changed his mind, and if so, had that wretched girl got anything to do with it?

'You can't do that!' Suzanne's face became set and hard as she recalled both the shocked words and the almost pleading look Fran had directed at Richard. And he had backed her up! She was not used to having her ideas challenged. Up to now whatever she did she had planned to do, willed it, and was in perfect command of the situation. Up to now. She looked at Fran, her eyes narrowed, and in that moment Fran realised with dismay that she had probably made a dangerous enemy.

CHAPTER NINE

FRAN found that, just as she had feared, Suzanne's presence at Brocade brought complications in its wake. Richard, with an obtuseness that surprised her, did not seem to realise that Suzanne was only happy when she was monopolising his entire attention and whenever chance brought him into the company of Fran and the children he made no attempt to simulate either boredom or disinterest. He also made it clear that he expected the pattern established over the preceding weeks to be continued, and was insistent that Fran should join himself and Suzanne for dinner and take her part in the conversation as a guest and as a friend.

If, Fran thought ruefully, he was trying to cement a friendship between Suzanne and herself his efforts were doomed to failure, for she was becoming increasingly conscious of the elder girl's unspoken hostility. She would have tried, in view of Richard's earlier request, to like Suzanne, but her patronising attitude made this extremely difficult. What would happen when Richard—who was taking a few days' holiday—again became immersed in his work she did not like to think. She certainly would not be able to help him by entertaining Suzanne, as he had suggested, and she could only hope that he would realise that this was not her fault. It was Suzanne, now, who treated her as an interloper, though she was careful not to do it so obviously that Richard would notice. He always appeared to be oblivious of the loaded atmosphere, though Fran, acutely uncomfortable, was usually glad to escape from the dinner table and spend the rest of the evening either alone or with Johnny and his mother.

Fran could not help regretting Suzanne's arrival, for since a better understanding had existed between Richard and herself life at Brocade had been so happy. Now everything, in some subtle way, had completely changed.

It was small consolation that Suzanne did not exactly endear herself to anyone. Her demands on the household put Mrs. Henderson in a dour mood—'She may have got servants waiting on her hand and foot in South Africa, but she hasn't got them here!—and the children cordially disliked her. They were quick to notice that she behaved quite differently to them when Richard was around than at any other time, and had the usual childish disdain of someone who was merely posing. (Funny, thought Fran, they'd cherished Richard even when he'd given every sign of disliking them, yet they were wholly contemptuous of Suzanne, who did at least pretend to like them!)

Johnny was another one who quickly saw through Suzanne's airs and graces. She had been charming enough to him at their first meeting—he was, after all, quite a personable young man, with his fair curly hair, laughing blue eyes and frank, pleasant manner— but her attitude quickly changed when she discovered that he was merely the son of the housekeeper. Luckily Johnny, with a University degree behind him and the prospect of a well-paid and attractive career in front of him, was amused rather than annoyed, but though he was never rude he made it quite clear that he was not a servant and did not intend to be treated like one.

'Mine host is in for a lively time if he marries that one,' he said to Fran with a slight grimace. 'I must say I gave him credit for more sense!'

'She's very beautiful,' Fran said, unwilling to admit that she wholeheartedly agreed.

Johnny shrugged. 'Handsome is as handsome does. I find her insufferable, but I admit that she may well appeal to someone in the champagne and caviare class.' He hesitated. He would have liked to have said more, but his mother had warned him to curb his unruly tongue and in any case he felt rather as though he might be treading on thin ice. He had never been able to decide what Fran's feelings were towards Richard, though he had a shrewd suspicion that even if she didn't realise it herself she had begun to get fond of him. As for Richard ... no, Johnny thought regretfully, he must have been quite wrong when he'd imagined that the master of Brocade had more than a cursory interest in his one-time unwanted guest. Fran was an absolute darling, but she didn't stand a chance against someone as well-equipped as Suzanne Pleydell. Just as well, perhaps. Quayle might easily make the very devil of a husband, and Fran was too sweet to be hurt. She was like his Eiluned ... loyal and steadfast, absolutely true. He hoped that one day the two girls would meet. They were bound to be friends, they were so much alike.

For most of the time Fran forced herself to ignore Suzanne's subtle antagonism and the tiny barbs she planted when Richard wasn't listening, but inevitably there came an evening when she found herself taking up the challenge, not on her own behalf but on the children's.

Richard had somehow discovered that it was Robin's birthday the following day and promptly suggested that to celebrate the occasion they should all picnic in the Cotswolds. Fran, conscious of Suzanne's frown, felt obliged to point out that there was not room even in Richard's large car for five children and three adults, but Richard had already foreseen this difficulty and brushed her objections aside.

'We'll include Johnny in the party,' he said in his

most autocratic manner. 'He's got a small car of his own, hasn't he? We'll manage quite easily with the two.'

This was so obviously true that Fran felt unable to argue, but Suzanne was put out and showed it.

'Robin? Oh, he's the one with that frightful scar, isn't he? I should think that instead of a picnic that child would benefit from a visit to a plastic surgeon!' she observed in her cool, brittle voice.

Fran stiffened. 'I don't think there's any need for plastic surgery. The scar will fade a lot in time.'

'Don't tell me your munificent Welfare State isn't willing to shoulder the expense,' Suzanne drawled. 'I was always under the impression that it was prepared to squander money left, right and centre on children whose parents are too idle or too feckless to shoulder the responsibility themselves.'

'The money isn't squandered. It's well spent.' Fran spoke with a dangerous quietness.

Suzanne shrugged. 'In some cases, perhaps. Personally I can think of worthier causes. In my opinion, where a child is in no danger of starvation or runs no risk of death or disfigurement the parents should be forced to face up to the problems they've created for themselves. There shouldn't be an easy get-out.'

Fran stared at her incredulously. 'And if the children are desperately unhappy?'

Suzanne shrugged again. 'Now you're going to get emotional. That's the worst of people like you. You always let sentiment cloud the issue.'

Richard sat watching them both, his face impassive. Fran's cheeks were flushed, her eyes sparkling with indignation. Suzanne's smug, unsympathetic attitude towards a problem she knew absolutely nothing about infuriated her and she answered her hotly.

'Economically as well as emotionally there's every reason why we should bother about unhappy children! There are good grounds for believing that severe emotional stress in childhood means, later on, either a prison sentence or intensive treatment in a mental hospital. Surely even you would agree that any steps taken to prevent delinquency or neurosis is a social investment for several generations ahead!' she flashed.

Suzanne's face was a study. Too late she realised that because Fran had taken great pains to be self-effacing, she had made the fatal mistake of under-estimating her. What was even more infuriating was that there was an unmistakable gleam of amusement in Richard's grey eyes.

She said coldly, 'I really don't feel inclined to argue about it. We're all entitled to our own opinions.'

She turned deliberately to Richard with a remark about something that had been in a letter she'd received that morning from her father, and Fran, who had missed that tell-tale gleam in Richard's eyes, felt an odd pang of disappointment. She hadn't expected him to champion her cause, and yet.... Somehow, listening to Suzanne's clear voice and Richard's answering, deep-toned and without its familiar mocking note, she felt hopelessly alone and shut out. Unwanted.

Robin's birthday dawned bright and clear. There were presents from everyone, including a boat from Mrs. Henderson, a football from Johnny, and a cow-boy outfit from Fran. Richard had not known in time to buy a gift, but there was a crisp pound note in the envelope he handed to the little boy, and Suzanne, not to be outdone, had added another ten shillings.

Robin, always the quietest of Fran's family, shy, and over-sensitive, was almost overwhelmed by such largesse. Fran, looking at his flushed cheeks and bright eyes, felt a rush of fierce possessive joy. Suzanne and people like her could say what they liked. Whatever it cost to make these children happy, it was worth it. She remembered Robin as he had been when she had first known him—much too small for his age, with a set, expressionless face and big, scared eyes, too cowed to make as much as a whimper. Even now, if ever Robin shouted or stamped his feet or banged a door she never felt able to reprove him ... the sound was music in her ears, after all those months of dumb passivity.

As she had expected, all the children were charmed by the idea of Robin's birthday treat. There was one snag inasmuch that Johnny had to be counted out of the party since he had an appointment at the hospital, but he willingly agreed to lend his small car to Fran. Danny, Robin and Mark piled in with her, while Beanie and Sue, placated with a promise that they could change places with the boys on the way home, travelled with Richard and Suzanne. Rather to Danny's disappointment, they were also in charge of the enormous picnic hamper packed by Mrs. Henderson.

Richard had already picked out the picnic spot, a lovely, secluded hillside he had remembered from his boyhood, and according to him, little changed. The children, Fran and Richard played cricket and rounders while Monday rushed around barking encouragement and Suzanne, pleading a weak ankle, watched with a faint air of thinly-disguised boredom. She looked, Fran thought, especially beautiful in a slim, sleeveless apricot-coloured dress which displayed her shapely limbs and exotic tan to the best possible advantage, and whatever she thought of Richard's philanthropic behaviour she was as charming to him as ever.

By tea-time, however, the charm had cracked a little and she ate practically none of the food so carefully prepared by Mrs. Henderson, though everyone else was ravenous.

'My dear!' she murmured, delicately arching her brows as Fran took a second sausage roll. (Mrs.

Henderson made heavenly, melt-in-the-mouth pastry.) 'Aren't you afraid of getting fat? I'd simply *die* if I put on even an extra *inch*!' Her complacent gaze flickered over her graceful slenderness: she knew quite well that she was at least a size smaller than Fran.

'I can't be bothered to diet,' Fran said equably. 'And being in the open air seems to give one such a terrific appetite!'

'Not me, it doesn't,' Suzanne said acidly. 'And really, all this starch...!' she sketched a little gesture of distaste.

Richard was laughing. 'Sorry, Suzanne, but you really can't expect poor Mrs. Henderson to reach Fortnum and Mason standards! Actually it's a jolly good spread—ask Danny! Have a hard-boiled egg, that's not fattening.'

'I loathe hard-boiled eggs,' Suzanne said coldly. This picnic was proving just as much of a bore as she had suspected it would be. She had very nearly elected to stay at home, but had eventually decided that this course of action would probably suit Fran only too well. Of course the wretched girl spent half her time making sheep's eyes at Richard, only he was such an idiot he didn't even notice it!

Fran was perhaps the only one who saw Richard's quick little frown. He made no comment, but it seemed to her that he made a deliberate effort to counteract Suzanne's rather blighting attitude. She could not help feeling grateful: it would have been a pity if Robin's treat had been spoiled.

After tea the children went exploring and Fran accompanied them, leaving Richard and Suzanne sitting side by side on the grass. The latter, addressing herself exclusively to Richard, was in the middle of a long and involved anecdote, her lovely oval face with its parted red lips raised in a provocatively charming gesture. It was fairly obvious, Fran thought, that she meant to keep Richard more or less anchored to her side from now on.

She glanced at the sky. She rather wished that she had had the foresight to bring raincoats, for although it had been fine when they set out from Brocade some dark clouds had since rolled up from nowhere and the sky now bore a somewhat threatening look. For a moment she hesitated, then she shrugged. They wouldn't be gone long, and anyway it was quite possible that the rain would hold off until after they got home. One could never predict the vagaries of the English weather.

Despite her optimism, however, the sky gradually became darker, and when they returned to the car, tired, breathless but exhilarated after a stiff climb, Richard was waiting for them, with Suzanne already in the car.

His gaze swept over the little group. 'Where's Monday?' He spoke rather more curtly than was necessary: it seemed as though some of his bonhomie had evaporated during their absence.

'Monday?' Fran looked round her in dismay as she realised for the first time that the puppy, who had certainly been with them as they started their homeward journey, was now nowhere to be seen.

'Well, for heaven's sake!' Suzanne said irritably. 'Couldn't *one* of you have kept an eye on him?' Her temper was very nearly at boiling point. Far from appearing to enjoy their tête-à-tête Richard had been maddeningly aloof. To cap it all she'd been stung by what she was sure had been a wasp, and instead of being decently solicitous Richard had laughed and told her it was merely a gnat bite. He wouldn't have been so unsympathetic if it had been one of those wretched brats, she thought bitterly.

'Monday! Monday! Come here, Monday!' Everyone started calling the puppy's name, but there was no response.

'We haven't lost him, have we?' Beanie asked, looking scared.

'We'd better go back and look for him,' Mark said, preparing to suit the action to the word, but Fran restrained him.

'There's no need for us all to go. I think I know where the little wretch has got to.' She looked apologetically at Richard. 'There's a fascinating rabbit hole up there and he didn't really want to leave it. I expect he shot back to it the moment we weren't looking.' She put her hand on Beanie's shoulder and pushed her gently towards Johnny's car. 'Go and get in, everyone. I won't be long.'

'I'll come with you. Let's hope the rain holds off till we get back.' Richard still sounded curt. Pausing only to sling a raincoat over his shoulder, he strode away up the hill without even waiting for her answer.

Annoyed with herself for her lack of vigilance, Fran followed, calling Monday's name, in vain, at intervals. Richard climbed in complete silence, his expression lowering. He had once told her, she recalled ruefully, that carelessness irritated him, and in this instance the carelessness was certainly hers.

It was with a sense of overwhelming relief that she presently discovered that she had been quite right about Monday's whereabouts. There he was, industriously digging and already almost hidden from view, only his eager, quivering tail advertising his illegal activities.

'Oh, Monday! You bad dog!' Fran scolded as ruthlessly Richard hauled him out. Monday gave a protesting yelp and squirmed indignantly in Richard's grasp, but knew when he was beaten. He hadn't seen much of his master since he had taken up residence at Brocade, but he had already learned that he'd better obey him—or else. (Not that Richard was ever unkind: Fran had discovered a long time ago that he had a soft spot for animals.)

'Go on, Monday! Scoot!' Richard commanded sternly. He glanced at the sky and then at Fran, and she realised with relief that whatever had caused his short temper he was not angry with her.

'We'd better hurry. It looks as though there's going to be a deluge at any moment.'

The threatening dark clouds were, indeed, almost overhead, and obediently Fran quickened her pace. Normally sure-footed, this time she tripped over a tuft of grass and went sprawling headlong.

'Fran! Are you all right?' She felt Richard's strong arms go round her, lifting her up, and for a moment, breathless and shaken, she leant her head against his shoulder. Then she looked up, and found that there was concern in his grey eyes which was completely at variance with the gruffness of his manner only a few moments before.

'I'm—all right. Just—winded,' she gasped, but she knew that it was not the shock of her fall which was causing the sudden wild beating of her heart. With every fibre of her being she was conscious of Richard's nearness, the firm clasp of his hands, and the steely strength of his lithe, muscular body. Suddenly, in a moment of revelation, the knowledge came to her that she loved this man ... had loved him for a long time, only she had never brought herself to admit it.

Time seemed to stand still. She heard Richard catch his breath, felt the sudden quick, nervous pressure of his hands. Then a large raindrop splashed on to her upturned face, and though it was only a drop it was as effective as a douche of cold water. Her cheeks flaming, she wrenched herself from his arms and jumped to her feet.

'Sorry about that! I tripped over a tuft of grass!' she flung breathlessly over her shoulder.

'You'll trip again if you keep up that breakneck speed,' Richard said mildly, lengthening his stride to keep up with her. There was an odd little smile in his grey eyes as he held out his raincoat. 'You'd better share this with me. It's raining quite fast now, or hadn't you noticed?'

'I'll be all right.' That wasn't strictly true, she thought ruefully; it was going to be a heavy shower.

'Do as you're told,' Richard spoke with a return to his old brusque manner. 'Who's going to look after the children if you go down with pneumonia?' He put his arm round her as he spoke and together they hurried to the car, their shoulders protected by the raincoat but the rain lashing their faces.

Fran did not even feel it. All she was conscious of was the warmth in her heart engendered by his nearness, but it was short-lived. The moment they got back to the car and she saw Suzanne's furious expression she was immediately jerked back to cold reality. For a few blissful moments she had almost forgotten Suzanne.

She drove home feeling as dishevelled mentally as she was sure she looked physically. She could not get herself orientated to her discovery that she was in love with Richard. It was a frightful complication. She hadn't wanted ever to love anyone again, not in that way, not after what Bryan had done to her. And to fall in love with someone like Richard was sheer madness! Cinderella and Prince Charming ... no, even if there'd been no Suzanne she wasn't quite silly enough to believe in *that* particular fairy story! Richard liked her ... perhaps even respected her a little ... but that was all.

She sighed, then her common sense reasserted itself and she laughed somewhat ruefully. Loving a person and not being loved in return wasn't necessarily a tragedy. She'd be content with Richard's friendship. 'Better half a loaf than no bread at all' ... that was one of her father's favourite sayings. She wondered, suddenly, what her parents would have thought of Richard. She'd always known that her father had had reservations about Bryan, though her mother had adored him. She'd been brokenhearted when their engagement had ended, and Fran had a shrewd suspicion that for ages she had clung to the forlorn hope that Bryan might realise he had made a terrible mistake. Funny ... she could think about Bryan absolutely dispassionately now. Had she ever been really in love with him ... or had she been merely swept off her feet by his charm and romantic good looks? This love she had for Richard was so different from the feeling she had had for Bryan. This went right into the marrow of her bones.

'Fran, I've asked you a question three times! Why don't you answer?' That was Beanie's plaintive voice, and with a sigh Fran abandoned her troubled thoughts, though they returned in full force later that evening, when the children were in bed.

Unable just at the moment to welcome the company of Johnny or his mother, she collected a cushion from the house and found herself a secluded spot on the terrace. It had stopped raining, but everywhere was still damp and the air smelt fresh and fragrant. She thought she would be undisturbed, but she had only been sitting there a few moments when she heard the sound of voices. First Suzanne's cool and brittle.

'I sincerely hope, Richard darling, that you don't intend to inflict anything else like this afternoon's entertainment on me? There's a limit, you know. Cast your bread upon the waters by all means, if that's what you feel like doing, but for goodness' sake don't expect me to be around when you do! I've never been so bored in all my life as I was at that dreadful picnic!'

There was a slight pause, then Fran, wondering frantically whether she should reveal her presence, heard Richard answer. There was a slight weariness in his voice, like that of an indulgent parent whose patience is tried.

'I'm sorry you didn't enjoy it, Suzanne. You'd better let me make it up to you. Is there anything you'd specially like to do tomorrow?'

'Well, there is, actually.' Suzanne sounded suddenly eager. 'Can we go to Stratford-on-Avon? It's not far, is it? There's a simply marvellous hotel there which used to be an Elizabethan manor house once: I thought if we saw it we might get some useful ideas for Brocade.'

To Fran's relief, they moved out of earshot. For a moment she sat very still. She had wondered whether Richard still intended to turn Brocade into a hotel, for on several occasions, when Suzanne had broached the subject, she had heard him turn her remarks aside. Evidently the project had not been forgotten, it had merely been shelved. She put her head between her hands and tried to reason herself out of her unhappiness. Neither Richard nor Brocade had anything to do with her. And yet.... She sighed again, picked up her cushion and went back into the house. Maybe Johnny would laugh her out of her melancholy mood ... as long as he didn't guess the reason for it!

She and the children were walking down the drive the next day when Richard's car passed them. Suzanne, beside him, smiled triumphantly. She had been having great difficulty in persuading Richard to take an enthusiastic interest in her plans for Brocade and she had had an uneasy suspicion that Fran was partly to blame. She'd obviously been filling his head with some romantic nonsense about his great heritage! It wasn't that he had actively opposed any of her ideas—save the one about the car park—but he was showing a marked disinclination to do anything about them. She longed to accuse him of having lost interest, but did not dare in case he admitted that this indeed was the case. Perhaps if he saw how successfully an old house could be converted into an hotel his enthusiasm would again be fired!

The plan was not as successful as she had hoped. On their return to Brocade he was so silent and preoccupied that after he had twice failed to answer a question she was driven to ask him point-blank what he had on his mind.

'I'm sorry. Was I distrait?' He smiled at her somewhat ruefully, regretting that he had had to be reminded of his obligations as host.

'You were, rather.' She regarded his profile thoughtfully. On a sudden impulse she asked, 'Richard, couldn't we spend a few days together in town? It's not that I'm bored with Brocade, I'm not, but—well, a change would be nice.'

'If you like.' Richard did not take his eyes off the road. He wished he could whip up more enthusiasm for her suggestion, but he was feeling oddly weary. Funny, he'd never realised before how demanding Suzanne was. It was almost impossible to relax in her presence and she seemed to talk incessantly. Not for Suzanne and himself were the companionable silences which were so often an important part of a good friendship.

He saw her mouth curling up in a satisfied little smile and added warningly, 'As long as you don't expect me to spend too much time with you, Suzanne. Things are in rather a bad way at our London branch: I'm beginning to wish I'd not left so much to old Hayley. He ought to have retired years ago: he was really past it, poor old boy. Someone's got to put in some pretty hard work before things get right again.'

Suzanne sat very still. Then she said softly, 'You aren't by any chance trying to tell me that the someone may well be you, are you, darling? I mean—you don't intend to become a fixture in London, do you?'

He shrugged. 'Why not? They could do well

enough without me in Johannesburg. No shortage of good men there.'

She let that pass. 'And Brocade? You *do* still mean to let me turn it into a first-class hotel, don't you?' She could not keep the indignation from her voice.

For a moment he was silent. Then, 'I don't know,' he said quietly. 'Quite honestly, Suzanne, I'm not sure, now, that it would be a good idea.'

'And I wonder,' Suzanne thought bitterly, 'just how much Fran Norton has got to do with that decision?' She said nothing, but her brain was working furiously. She wasn't beaten yet.

CHAPTER TEN

SUZANNE's departure from Brocade was greeted with relief by everyone.

'Perhaps she won't come back again,' Mark said hopefully. He had once seen Suzanne slapping poor Monday—*hard*—just because he'd jumped up at her, and he hadn't even had muddy paws, her silly old dress wasn't marked at all!

'Don't be silly. She's got to come back. She's going to marry Mr. Quayle,' Robin said mournfully.

There was dead silence while the rest of the children digested this unwelcome piece of information.

Then—'Is she really? Gosh, what a pity!' said Danny with devastating frankness.

'How do you know she's going to marry him?' Beanie demanded. 'He hasn't given her a ring!' She appealed to Fran. 'Don't you have to have a ring if you're going to get married to someone, Fran?'

'Well ... it's usual, but not necessary,' Fran told her. Her voice and face were serene, but Mrs. Henderson gave her a sharp look. Johnny was not the only one who had begun to suspect that Richard Quayle was becoming smitten with Fran's charms, though unlike Johnny Mrs. Henderson had known when to hold her tongue. She regretted, anyway, that her suspicions appeared to have been unfounded. Certainly Suzanne Pleydell was beautiful, but the housekeeper resented her sharp tongue and overbearing ways and thought 'Mr. Richard' would be a fool if he married her. She gave a wry smile, for she'd just thought of an old rhyme she'd once read, and which seemed singularly apposite.

> 'The lad who'll pass
> A good sweet lass
> For one whose temper bristles,
> He is a fool, for he will pass
> Through corn to get to thistles.'

'Mr. Richard' would find the thistles all right, for all that Suzanne took such good care to smile sweetly at him now!

Fran herself was fairly certain that Richard meant to marry Suzanne, though at times she had had the feeling that if what was going on between Richard and Suzanne was a love affair, it didn't appear to be making either of them very happy. Suzanne's beautiful face habitually wore a rather sullen expression and Richard's temper was ragged. Somehow she couldn't imagine them married. It was not, she was quite sure, her own love for Richard which made her dislike Suzanne so much. She seemed entirely to lack human warmth, and though Margot had once suggested that temperamentally she and her cousin were well suited, Fran was quite convinced that Richard's coldness and cynicism was nothing but a surface veneer ... a kind of protective coating ... and that underneath it all he was kind and warm and considerate. He didn't deserve a fate like Suzanne!

During the few days' respite before Richard and his visitor were due to return to Brocade, life slipped back into its gentle, peaceful pattern. Fran tried with all her might to keep Richard out of her mind, but was only partially successful. He stayed with her like a persistent ghost, and she was powerless to dismiss the bitter-sweet memories his image evoked. It might have been worse, she thought, had it not been for Johnny. Sometimes she wondered how much he had guessed. Never by look or word did he trespass, but he made every effort to help her and she was warmed and comforted by the mere fact of his friendship.

On one particularly lovely day Miss Challoner drove down to see them for the first time. She was sorry to have missed Richard, but she enthused over Brocade and exclaimed delightedly when she saw how well and happy the children were looking.

'I'm almost afraid to tell you that I think No. 17 will be ready for you in about ten days' time,' she said laughingly. 'The builders seem to have got a move on at last.' She looked thoughtfully around her. A faint breeze was stirring the leaves of the trees and sunshine and shadow chased each other across the lawn. 'The children will miss all this badly, won't they?'

Not only the children. Fran felt her heart sink, not so much at the prospect of leaving Brocade, though she loved it, but because she would never see Richard again. Ships that passed in the night ... only Richard was so much more than a ship, he was a beacon in the darkness, and when it was switched off she knew that she would feel lonelier than she had ever felt in her life before. The pain of Bryan's betrayal would be as nothing compared with the anguish of losing Richard. She realised now that most of her unhappiness when Bryan had broken their engagement was not because she had loved him very deeply, but because she had trusted him and he had let her down so badly. But Richard....

Beanie had come up to stand at their side, her plain, heart-shaped little face with its large hazel eyes very serious. With an effort Fran jerked herself back to the present. She'd always known that she would lose Brocade and Richard eventually. It was just going to happen a little sooner than she had expected, that was all.

'Miss Challoner, have you been to see my mummy? Is she getting better now?'

Fran caught her breath. Beanie and Danny prayed every night for their mother's recovery but it was only the other night that Danny remarked, sadly, that it seemed to be taking God a long time to say yes. Perhaps they should have warned that there wasn't a chance ... and yet how could one be so brutally frank with children so young? And miracles *did* happen—sometimes.

Miss Challoner's voice was very gentle. 'No, I'm afraid I haven't seen her, Beanie. She's very, very ill, you know that. Too ill for visitors.'

Beanie nodded. 'I know. I just wondered.'

She spoke bravely, but her face was wistful, and Fran spoke quickly.

'Beanie, do you think you could go and find Monday for me? Miss Challoner is longing to see him.'

Beanie's face brightened and she ran off obediently. Miss Challoner sighed.

'Poor Beanie. It won't be long now, I'm afraid. The last report I had was definitely not encouraging.'

'It's very hard,' Fran said pitifully.

'Yes.' Miss Challoner regarded her intently. She had bracketed Fran with the children when she'd said how well and happy they all looked, but now she was beginning to wonder if she'd made a mistake. Certainly Fran was glowing with health, but there were faint blue stains under her eyes and a wistful curve to her mouth. No, Miss Challoner thought, there was something wrong but since it didn't seem to concern any of the children then it was Fran's own affair, and she had no intention of prying or probing.

Fran did not tell the children that they would soon be returning to London: there was no point in meeting trouble half-way. Parting with Monday, of course, was going to be the biggest heartache. The puppy was growing fast and was bright-eyed and mischievous, with alert, silken ears and an ingratiating tail. He adored the children, and they were his devoted slaves. Following Richard's instructions, they fed him, brushed him, played with him, scolded him a little, talked to him and took him for long walks come wind, come weather.

It was on one such walk, just after Miss Challoner's visit, that Monday proved that for all his puppy lovableness he had also inherited his fair share of aggressive instincts.

Mrs. Henderson had asked Fran if they would mind taking a note to one of the daily helps, who lived in a cottage at the far end of the village. It was a long walk, but all the children were eager to go, for it was not very often that they went through the village. For one thing, Monday had to be kept on a lead because of the traffic and for another there was usually an argument as to whose turn it was to hold it!

En route for the cottage they had to pass the Coates' rambling old house, and they saw Rosemary, trim and neat in slacks and a butcher-blue shirt, working in the front garden. At the sound of children's voices she looked up, hesitated, then raised her hand in a brief salute before returning with redoubled energy to her digging. Watching her, Fran remembered something that Michael had said about his wife ... 'Since she can't have children she lavishes all her affection on her garden. At least her plants are growing things.'

Beanie, who had claimed her turn to hold Monday's lead and who was walking slightly ahead of the others, looked at the house with interest. It seemed a nice friendly place, she thought. Not half as big and beautiful as Brocade, of course, but—nice. She was just wondering what it was like inside when suddenly she felt a violent tug on the lead. Monday, up until then a model of decorum, had caught sight of a big black cat sitting by the side of the road and sedately washing its face. It didn't look in the least like the scrawny Matilda, but it was certainly a member of the feline species, and Monday considered *all* cats legitimate prey.

With a loud bark he bounded forward and Beanie,

running to keep up with him, fell headlong on the dusty road. With an exclamation of dismay Fran rushed forward to pick her up. She was sobbing bitterly, for it had been a nasty fall, and her hands, knees and face were badly grazed.

'Darling, don't cry!' Fran tried desperately to mop up the tears and staunch the blood which was trickling from the poor little button nose.

'What a mess!' said Robin sympathetically, and proffered his own somewhat disreputable-looking pocket handkerchief.

'I've got Monday!' Mark panted. He gave the puppy an admonishing pat. 'Just *look* what you've done to poor Beanie! You *know* you're not supposed to chase cats!'

'I'm hurting all over!' Beanie wailed. Danny, trying frantically to think of something to bring her comfort, mutely held out his two very best coloured marbles, but Beanie was crying too hard even to notice.

'What on earth is the matter?' Rosemary, hearing Beanie's anguished sobs, had emerged from her garden, and took in the situation at a glance.

'Oh dear! You *have* had a tumble! What happened?' she asked with ready sympathy.

'Monday pulled Beanie over,' three or four voices informed her in unison.

'My goodness, look at those poor old hands and knees!' Rosemary exclaimed. She looked at Fran. 'You'd better all come with me. Luckily Michael's at home: he'll look after Beanie. She can't possibly walk home in that state.' She smiled at the sobbing child. 'Don't cry, Beanie! When the doctor's bandaged you up I'll see if I can find you something nice.' She glanced round at the small concerned faces and added, 'You too.'

Fran's relief was evident. 'Are you sure you don't mind? I'd like Michael to look at these grazes, they're really rather severe, but there's no earthly reason why you should be bothered with all of us.'

'Don't be silly, Fran!' Rosemary sounded impatient. 'Beanie's been hurt and you all look a bit shaken. Come on, do! Hold on to Monday, Mark, we don't want him going off on high jinks again!' and chatting in a friendly, reassuring way to Beanie she shepherded the children into the house.

Fran, who was rather more worried about the extent of the grazing than she would have cared to admit, carried Beanie into Michael's surgery for treatment, leaving the boys with Rosemary. Michael, with the skill and gentleness which endeared him to all his small patients, carefully cleansed away the dirt and applied some sticking plaster. Then he looked at Fran.

'I suppose she's had the usual routine immunisation against tetanus? Then in that case all that's needed is a booster.'

The injection was given with the minimum of fuss and bother.

'Good girl, Beanie!' Michael approved. He swung the child up into his arms. 'Where are the others, Fran? You haven't left them outside?'

'They're with Rosemary.' Fran's eyes met his over Beanie's head. 'She insisted that we all came in.'

She saw him make a surprised move towards the door and spoke quickly, guided by an odd intuition.

'Michael, do you think perhaps it might be better if you stayed here? It might be—easier—for Rosemary.'

For a moment he looked startled, then he nodded. 'You're probably right. Goodbye, Beanie! Tell your brother you were a very brave girl and that he can be proud of you!'

Rosemary was kneeling on the floor of her sitting room, Monday on her lap, when Fran and Beanie went in. She was surrounded by Mark, Robin, Danny and Sue, who were patting and stroking the puppy, munching chocolate biscuits and drinking lemonade from tall, multi-coloured glasses. They looked perfectly at home and Rosemary, Fran noted with relief, was laughing at something one of them had said.

She got up immediately she saw Fran and Beanie and put the puppy down beside the children. Immediately he wagged his tail, gave a short, commanding bark and eyed Mark's biscuit longingly.

'Greedy little thing!' said Rosemary severely. 'You've had four already, and they aren't at all good for your figure or your teeth!' She smiled at Beanie. 'I've got some lemonade for you, Beanie, and I think I've managed to save you a few biscuits as well. Are you feeling better now?'

'The doctor stuck a needle into me and I didn't cry one bit,' Beanie said proudly. She looked round the sitting room with interest, glad to discover that the inside of the house was just as nice as she'd thought it might be.

'Isn't this a pretty room? I like it.'

'I'm glad,' Rosemary said quietly. She brought Beanie her lemonade and then sat talking to all the children for several more minutes, answering their questions and revealing an instinctive understanding of small children which somehow hurt Fran unbearably. She was the kind of person who would have been in her element as the mother of a large family—she would have taken all its problems in her stride. What a waste, she thought—and then found comfort in the reflection that whatever her feelings about 'other people's children' Rosemary had put them aside in order to give help and comfort when it was needed. It was only a small beginning, but if it really *was* a beginning then, perhaps, one day....

'I wish we could go there again,' Beanie said wistfully when they left.

'She hasn't got any children of her own. Perhaps she'll ask us to tea one day,' Robin said hopefully. 'Those biscuits were scrummy!'

Fran's face was thoughtful. Rosemary tried to pretend that she had no love to give and that she wished to receive none. But it was only a pretence, and today she had revealed the first chinks in her armour.

The next day Suzanne returned unexpectedly to Brocade, and alone. She seemed to be in a very disgruntled mood and it was obvious that whatever she had had in mind when she suggested to Richard that they spend a few days in town, her plans had miscarried.

In actual fact she had seen very little of Richard. Her intention had been to get him away from Brocade, where it seemed to her that any kind of intimacy was impossible because of Fran and the children, but she had soon discovered that in London the situation was far worse. As her host at Brocade Richard had felt himself obliged to put himself at her disposal: in London there were too many diversions for him to consider that necessary. Consequently she had had to amuse herself most of the time and she was in a thoroughly bad mood in consequence.

Her only slight consolation had come when they had dined with Margot and her husband. The former had made no secret of the fact that she strongly disapproved of any plan to turn Brocade into a hotel, but Richard, much to Suzanne's relief, had refused to be drawn into an argument. Evidently, she'd thought with satisfaction, he had by no means made up his mind to abandon the whole project. He was still dithering, and one little push in the right direction, given at the right time....

At any rate she had been sufficiently encouraged to do quite a lot of groundwork, though naturally she had had to keep quiet about her activities in that direction. Tessa Ryan, a South African friend now working in London, had introduced her to Julian Bentall, a young architect who had happened to

145

mention that he had converted several very old houses into country clubs or hotels. They had talked at length about Brocade and she had been intrigued by his approach. She badly wanted Richard to meet him, but realised that she would have to use a certain amount of guile: Richard would not thank her for making his decisions for him. Then Tessa had mentioned casually that Julian was taking her to a big charity ball at the Dorchester and had suggested that she and Richard join their party. Suzanne had jumped at the idea. All she had to do now was to sell it to Richard at some appropriate time. Though goodness knew when that would be. She'd quite thought that he had meant to return with her to Brocade, but at the last moment he had rung her up to say he couldn't make it until the following day. Brocade without Richard to take the edge off its deadly dullness! She pulled a face. She'd die of boredom!

Suzanne, as Fran learnt later, had her own methods of dispelling boredom. She occupied herself by giving gratuitous advice to Mrs. Henderson and old Sam, listened to in polite silence by the former but with mounting indignation by the latter. In his beloved garden Sam was as much of an autocrat as Richard in his different sphere.

'I really thought the poor old chap was going to burst a blood vessel,' Johnny, who had been an onlooker, told Fran, chuckling. 'He was as red as a turkey cock and so was my lady, by the time he'd finished! He told her he'd been gardening for upwards of fifty years and didn't need any know-it-all from foreign parts to tell him what to do! She was furious, but she had the sense to keep quiet and let the storm roll over her head.'

'I hope she won't make trouble for Sam when Richard comes home,' Fran said anxiously.

'She may try, but I doubt if she'll succeed. The old chap's a damned good gardener, for all his surly ways. Mind you, Suzanne poked her nose in at the worst possible moment. He's feeling like the devil, though he's too proud to admit it. Lumbago. It nearly kills him to bend.'

'Oh, I'm sorry,' Fran said with instant sympathy. She had seen very little of Sam since Mark's fall from grace, but it had seemed to her that he was gradually becoming resigned to their presence at Brocade. Certainly he had seemed a little less taciturn of late.

She realised the truth of Johnny's words the following day when she saw Sam at work. His weatherbeaten face was drawn with pain and he was hobbling around with obvious difficulty. It was no surprise to her when at lunchtime she learned from Mrs. Henderson that he had finally been forced to give in to his relentless enemy and go home.

'He started trying to weed the drive,' the housekeeper said grimly. 'Of all the silly, stubborn old fools! That drive's half a mile long if it's a yard. He won't use weed killer, either. Says it's unnatural.'

After a moment Mark touched Fran's arm. His face had gone very red. 'Could we finish weeding the drive for Sam, Fran?'

Startled, Fran looked first at him, then at Mrs. Henderson. She said doubtfully, 'It would be very hard work, Mark.'

Mark scuffed his toe along the ground. 'I don't mind.'

He was trying to make amends for the damage he had caused to the old man's plants, Fran realised with a quick flash of intuition. She said quietly, 'All right. We'll all do some weeding this afternoon, instead of going for a walk.'

'Me, too?' Sue demanded, and Fran laughed.

'You can help push the wheelbarrow!' she said,

ruffling the blonde curls.

Throughout the long, hot afternoon she and the children toiled at their self-appointed task. It was not especially difficult since the weeds were fairly sparse and the roots came out easily, but the drive was a long one and towards the end everyone's back was aching badly.

They were returning to the house, glowing with the satisfaction of a job well done, when they met Suzanne. Fran noticed that she was doing her hair a different way—it looked even more elegant than before. And she was wearing a new lipstick which emphasised more than ever the contrast between her white skin and black hair.

She raised her eyebrows when she saw their grubby hands and the tools which Fran was carrying.

'Been gardening? I hope you asked permission first!' she said acidly.

'As a matter of fact we didn't. Sam's gone home with a bad attack of lumbago. We've merely finished some weeding for him,' Fran told her.

Suzanne gave a disagreeable little laugh. 'I can't think why Richard doesn't pension the old boy off. He's not a scrap of real use: much too slow and shaky.'

Fran's eyes sparkled indignantly. When Suzanne's barbs were directed at her she bore them with equanimity, but she could not tolerate her unjust attacks on other people.

'I think Sam does a marvellous job. He certainly has the knack of making things grow, and he loves his work.'

Suzanne's eyes narrowed. She said coolly, 'Well, I'm afraid there'll have to be some changes before long. When this place is run on a commercial basis there won't be room for sentimentality.'

'On a commercial basis?' Fran echoed her words blankly.

'Why, yes. You know, of course, that Richard intends to turn Brocade into a hotel? You surely didn't think he'd changed his mind?' Suzanne asked in a brittle tone. She took her cigarette case out of her pocket and lit a cigarette. 'In point of fact renovations would have already been under way, but you and the children'—her hard eyes flickered over the silent group—'are the fly in the ointment. I don't suppose Richard would ever tell you so, but the fact is he can't proceed until you've gone. There's a lot of preliminary planning and an awful lot of work involved, you know.'

Fran had gone white. Suzanne spoke with such calm assurance that it never occurred to her to doubt the truth of what she'd said. So much for her hopes that Brocade had been reprieved!

She said a little unsteadily, 'I'm sorry that our presence here has held things up. Fortunately our own home will be ready for us very shortly.'

'Good. I expect you'll be glad to get back to your own environment, won't you?' Suzanne said sweetly.

It was Johnny who saved Fran from answering. He had come up behind her and took the tools from her hands.

'Mother asked me to tell you that tea's ready. I'll put these away for you. You and the kids have done a grand job: old Sam'll be as pleased as punch, though I don't suppose he'll say so,' he said laughingly.

Suzanne did not miss the warmth in his voice nor the quick look of gratitude Fran shot at him. She puffed thoughtfully at her cigarette, a sudden vague idea taking shape in her mind. It might be a great help if Richard could be brought to believe that there was something between Fran and Johnny Henderson. It was impossible that Richard had really fallen for that little nonentity but she had an uneasy feeling that he was definitely attracted. If so, it would explain a lot of things ... why, for instance, he was keeping her, Suzanne, at arm's length.

She stayed where she was for some moments, watching the little group cross the lawn. Then she followed, still deep in thought.

CHAPTER ELEVEN

HAD Miss Challoner seen Fran the next day she would have been more convinced than ever that there was something wrong. She had spent a restless night and her shadowed eyes and pale, drawn face testified to that fact.

What Suzanne had said had been an unpleasant shock. Richard's attitude seemed to have changed so completely towards her and the children that she had had no idea that he might still regard their continued presence at Brocade as an embarrassment. He had said that he was happy for them to stay as long as they wished, and because of his increased friendliness she had been foolish enough to think that he meant it. But now that Suzanne had pointed it out she realised that they must indeed have been a fly in the ointment. Of course if he were contemplating extensive structural alterations to his house he would find his six uninvited guests very much in the way. She only wished that she had realised that for herself ... it had been humiliating to have it pointed out by Suzanne. And humiliating to have to face up to the fact that she had fooled herself into thinking that perhaps the magic of Brocade had laid its spell upon him as well as upon her. She felt tired and depressed. Did being in love mean that one was always a prey to illusions?

At any rate, she thought a little bitterly, she would be able to give Richard the glad news of their imminent departure directly he got home. She wondered how he would react. Probably he would express polite regret ... but of course he wouldn't really be sorry. When they had gone he and Suzanne would be able to proceed with their plans, unhindered and uninterrupted. Brocade as she had known and loved it would be no more....

She blinked back the tears which blurred her eyes. Richard must never know that she cared for him. Apart from anything else, she felt instinctively that it would trouble him if he knew that she had allowed her emotions to get out of hand. For all his apparent cynicism, she had learned that he was sensitive to other people's hurts.

The one person she felt she could not face was Suzanne, who was mooning about the house unwilling to admit to anyone that she did not quite know when Richard would be returning. She made so many demands on Mrs. Henderson's time that the latter's routine was severely disrupted and she accepted gratefully when Fran offered to dust and do the flowers.

Not that Fran regarded either task as a chore. Secure in the knowledge that the children were playing happily, she passed the best part of two hours in keen enjoyment, bent on giving each room a delicious scheme of colour—nothing must jar. Had Sam been back at work she would have found her choice of flowers limited, for he always complained bitterly whenever his precious plants were cut and guarded them jealously from Mrs. Henderson's predatory scissors. In his absence, however, Fran was able to cut all that she wanted, and she was just arranging some particularly choice blooms as centrepiece for a gate-legged table in the library when a deep, achingly familiar voice spoke from behind her.

'I wondered when I came through the hall whose deft fingers had been at work!'

It was Richard. Completely absorbed in her task, she had not heard the car. She had not known, either, that he was coming home today and, taken by surprise, she took a few quick steps towards him before she could stop herself. She had not seen him for so long, and she had missed him so much, that the joy was blazing out in her eyes and her cheeks were as pink as the flowers in her hand. Suddenly her depression had rolled away. The mere sight of him was enough to make her heart sing.

For a moment they looked at each other in silence, then he came across to her and gently cupped her face in his hands.

'Oh, Fran!' was all that he said, but the light in his grey eyes made her pulse race wildly.

An icy voice spoke from the doorway.

'Welcome home, darling.'

Suzanne stood there, her hands in the pockets of her cherry-red dress, watching them. She looked beautiful but formidable, like a dark, avenging angel.

Richard released Fran without haste and smiled at Suzanne. The warmth in his eyes had given way to a kind of wariness, but when he spoke his voice was calm and friendly.

'Hello, Suzanne.'

Ignoring Fran completely, she walked over to him and laid her hand upon his sleeve in an intimate, proprietorial gesture. Whatever her feelings, she had them well under control.

'I'm so glad you're home, darling. I've got such heaps to tell you. I've missed you badly.'

It was beautifully done, her air of eager, almost childlike excitement. Richard hesitated, his glance going from her to Fran, but before he had a chance to speak she had already started to walk towards the door.

'I must hurry. There's still the drawing room to do,' she said quietly. The colour had ebbed from her face now, leaving her even paler than before.

'The flowers look quite pretty.' Suzanne's smile was patronising. 'I suppose you've got a flair for doing that sort of thing.'

Richard said quickly, 'I'll see you later, Fran. I've

brought home a few oddments for the children.'

'Thank you. It was nice of you to think of them,' Fran said, still in the same quiet voice. She went out into the hall, shutting the door behind her, but just before she did so she saw Suzanne put her hands on Richard's shoulders and lift her lovely, glowing face to his. She leant for a moment against the wall, feeling as though something inside her was weeping slow tears. It just wasn't true, she thought desolately, about half a loaf being better than no bread at all. Oh, it might work for some people, but not for her. All she was doing was eating her heart out for the other half ... the half she could never have. It was Suzanne whom Richard loved, and the expression she thought she had seen in his grey eyes just now must have been no more than a trick of the light.

She did not see Richard again until after tea, when accompanied by Suzanne he gave the children the 'oddments' he had mentioned. In fact these turned out to be a number of delightful and obviously expensive toys which took everyone's breath away.

'Heavens, they'll think it's Christmas!' Suzanne said in what Fran suspected was feigned amusement. 'Still, until they get broken they'll serve as souvenirs of your stay at Brocade, won't they, Fran?'

'Souvenirs?' Richard's voice was sharp. 'Why souvenirs?'

Fran answered him steadily. 'We shall be leaving Brocade very shortly, Richard. Miss Challoner drove down while you were away to tell me that our own home is almost ready for us.'

She turned away as she spoke, bending over Sue so that she wouldn't have to see the inevitable flash of relief in Richard's eyes. He'd be pleased, of course. How could he help it?

He said nothing, however, and when she next looked at him his face was, as ever, inscrutable. She smiled and made polite conversation, but all the time she felt as though the aching inside her would never stop.

In her desolation she sought out Johnny, longing for the comfort of his unfailing kindness and cheerful good humour. At the moment he was in especially good form, for he had had a letter from Eiluned saying that her father was so much better that she had hopes of returning to England in the very near future.

'I want an autumn wedding,' he told Fran as together they walked towards the home meadow, which had come to occupy a specially warm place in her affection for Brocade. 'I don't suppose I'll get anyone else to want it, though. Eiluned says she's got to get her trousseau ready, and as for Mum...! She does nothing but pull a long face and quote ridiculous proverbs about marrying in haste, repenting at leisure. She doesn't know Eiluned or she'd not act so daft!'

Fran laughed, looking at him with amused affection. 'Well, of course that's the trouble, Johnny. She doesn't know Eiluned. And three months ago neither did you.'

'*You* aren't suggesting that I don't know my own mind, are you?' Johnny asked with mock indignation. 'It took me only five seconds flat to decide Eiluned was the girl for me, but then I agree with Shakespeare. "Who ever lov'd that lov'd not at first sight?"'

No, thought Fran wryly, that wasn't always so. She'd disliked Richard intensely at their first meeting: love in her case had come gradually, finally catching her unawares.

Aloud she said lightly, 'Well, you can't expect your mother to go along with that. She was telling me the other night that she and your father were "walking out" for nearly four years before they decided to get married, and even then she had last-minute qualms because she was afraid she didn't know him well enough!

The sound of their laughter drifted across the still air to where Richard was walking with Suzanne. It was only with difficulty that she had prised him out of the house: he had claimed that he had important letters to write but had finally yielded to her persuasions. In actual fact she was feeling almost desperate. She could not prolong her stay at Brocade indefinitely and it seemed to her that since his return from London he had retreated even further into a bank of reserved politeness. She had a feeling that he had definitely made up his mind that Brocade was not to be turned into a hotel and that it would not be long before he told her so. Angry and resentful, for Richard was the one man she had wanted and not been able to get, she laid the blame at one person's door—Fran Norton's. She was now absolutely sure that Fran meant more to Richard than at the moment he was prepared to confess, and the knowledge was gall and wormwood. The little housemother to succeed where she, Suzanne, brilliant and beautiful, had failed! Not, she thought grimly, if she could possibly help it!

At the sight of Fran and Johnny together her eyes gleamed. Here was her chance.

'I rather think something is brewing between our little housemother and the housekeeper's handsome son, don't you?' she observed carelessly. 'Look at them now! Talk about love's young dream!'

Just at that moment Fran had climbed the gate leading into the meadow and was sitting at the top, looking down at Johnny and laughing. As Richard followed Suzanne's gaze Johnny held out his arms and swung her down. He would have released her immediately, but a strand of her long fair hair had become entangled around one of the buttons on his jacket and it took him several moments to free it. Richard, too far away to see exactly what had happened, drew a short breath and his heavy brows came together in a startled frown.

Then he said shortly, 'Nonsense. You're letting your imagination run away with you. Johnny and Fran are just good friends. He's been very kind to the children, I believe: he's fond of them, and that in itself is sufficient recommendation for Fran.'

Suzanne's expression was one of amused disbelief.

'Darling, you're terribly obtuse sometimes! Still...!' She shrugged as if to say that the matter was not important. She was clever enough not to overplay her hand.

Richard was still frowning. In spite of himself he found himself watching as Fran and Johnny crossed the meadow. Fran was wearing a blue dress and the shining fall of her hair was a burnished gold in the evening sunlight. Johnny, beside her, had an air of vitality, a zest for living, which the older man suddenly noticed and envied.

Suzanne was watching him, not Fran and Johnny. Realising this, he turned sharply.

'I'm going back to the house. Coming?' he threw over his shoulder, and Suzanne, a tiny smile curling the corners of her beautiful provocative mouth, complied.

Sam returned to work the following day. He was still somewhat bowed and moved a little stiffly, but it appeared that the worst of the attack was over. A hot iron on his back, he told Mrs. Henderson, had worked wonders—'better'n all they pills the doctor dishes out!'

He was clearly suspicious about what had, and what had not, been done in his absence, but according to Johnny he was hard put to it not to show downright relief that the drive had been tidied. Fran had not expected any sign of appreciation and was taken by surprise when Sam stopped her to say a few gruff words of thanks.

'It was Mark's idea,' Fran told him. She hesitated. 'You know, Sam, he really is sorry about what he did to your plants.'

'So I should think, the young varmint!' Sam spoke with all his usual truculence, and Fran sighed. Evidently, she thought, Mark was not going to be forgiven. She was sorry: she would have liked to have been able to feel that when they departed from Brocade they would leave nothing but goodwill behind them. She said as much to Johnny, but he only laughed.

'Sam's bark is a lot worse than his bite. He doesn't go in for pretty speeches, but he did tell me to let you know that he's lighting a big bonfire this evening, after tea, and you and the children are welcome to watch. That, from Sam, is the nearest thing to an olive branch you'll get.'

A bonfire! Yes, the children would love that. She'd wanted to make them one on Guy Fawkes Night last year, but it had been out of the question: the garden at No. 17 was much too small. She realised, with a sudden pang, that November was not so far away. The summer was almost over. Already the countryside showed signs of the first mellow fruitfulness of autumn. In the fields around Brocade the harvesters were at work, and in the orchards ripening apples hung on the trees.

The passing of each season always saddened her a little, though she knew it was inevitable. You had to let the summer go, take autumn to your heart, learn to love it and then let it go in turn as winter's icy fingers gripped. Winter ... what was it Margot had said? 'Be thankful you're here at Brocade in the summer. It's the coldest and draughtiest house imaginable in winter.' She couldn't really believe that. The heart of Brocade would always warm the people within its walls. And it hurt her a little that she would never know what Brocade looked like under a moonwashed winter sky, with frost sparkling on the roof and silvering the bare branches of the trees, and with holly berries glowing in the copse.

She could always come back, of course, but it would never be the same. It wasn't just that she could not bear the thought of seeing Brocade as a hotel. She also knew quite well that once he had put the necessary work in hand it was unlikely that Richard would stay in England. He would appoint a well-trained and competent staff to look after his interests and return with Suzanne to sunny South Africa. Probably he'd then proceed to forget all about the old house nestling in the heart of the Cotswolds ... at least until it was time to study the annual balance sheet! Perhaps, if Suzanne hadn't come.... She sighed and tried to push her tangled thoughts away, but later that evening, when she stood with the children around Sam's bonfire they returned in full force.

Mark, Robin and Danny were helping Johnny to collect the twigs and dead branches which Sam was anxious to burn. Beanie and Sue, standing well back, had rapt expressions, as if they were half mesmerised by the beauty of the leaping flames. Fran was thankful that for them, at least, the sparking of the wood and the curling smoke with its licking tongues of crimson seemed to bring back no hideous memories of that dreadful night. In her case the nightmare still lingered: even now sometimes she would wake up, shuddering, with the smell of smoke in her nostrils and the greedy roar of the flames crackling in her ears.

Johnny, his shoulders looking broader than ever in the thick, loose polo-necked sweater he was wearing, flung some damp and rotting leaves on to the golden heart of the fire. Immediately dense clouds of livid white smoke billowed out, enveloping Fran, who was nearest, in an acrid blanket which made her cough and splutter and her eyes smart and sting.

'Oh, sorry, Fran!' Johnny flung a sympathetic arm

around her shoulders and drew her away. 'I should have warned you to stand further back.'

'You certainly should!' Still choking, blinded by smoke, Fran buried her face on his shoulder, the rough wool of his jersey pricking her cheeks. Johnny held her, his expression rueful, until her paroxysm of coughing had ceased.

'All right?' He grinned down at her as she lifted her head, 'You'd better go and stand with Sue and Beanie. I don't want to asphyxiate you.'

'I'll certainly move out of the danger zone!' she said with a laugh, and walked over to where she had positioned Sue and Beanie. Then and only then did she realise that they were not alone. They were talking nineteen to the dozen to Richard, and as she caught sight of his slightly raised brows and the enigmatic expression on his dark face she found herself blushing furiously. How long had he been standing there? Glad that her heightened colour could be explained by the glow of the fire, she tried hard to appear completely casual.

'What's this? Premature Guy Fawkes celebrations?' Richard asked coolly.

'Not really. But there's something irresistible about a bonfire, isn't there?' she said, matching his tone.

'Obviously.' There was a note of dryness in his voice for which she was at a loss to account. He thrust his hands deep into his pockets, his sombre gaze on the leaping flames which threw a fitful light over Johnny's tall figure and Sam's bowed one as they worked.

Beanie plucked at his arm.

'Mr. Quayle, did Fran tell you we've got to go back to London next week? I wish we didn't have to,' she said sadly.

'Oh, but you'll have other holidays in the country some time,' Richard comforted her. Fran saw that his face had softened: he could be so gentle when he chose.

'Here?' Beanie looked at him hopefully.

Richard hesitated and Fran intervened quickly. 'Darling, I've already explained to you about that.' She met Richard's eyes. 'I'm afraid they'll find London an awful let-down after the freedom they've enjoyed here.'

'And you? Will you be glad or sorry to dispense with my hospitality?'

Fran thought the grey eyes mocked her and pride made her toss back a rejoinder in equally flippant vein.

'I shall miss Mrs. Henderson's cooking, perhaps.'

He was silent, and she was aware of an odd constraint between them. It hurt and puzzled her, that barrier: it had not been there before.

Then he said: 'Talking about cooking—I'm taking Suzanne out to dinner tonight. Mrs. Henderson can reserve her heavy artillery for tomorrow—some friends from South Africa are spending the night here and Suzanne seems to think they'll expect something pretty special in the way of food. I hope Mrs. Henderson will be able to rise to the occasion.'

'I'm sure she will.'. What on earth were they doing, talking like polite strangers?

He hesitated again. 'You're perfectly welcome to join the party, Fran, but you may feel a little out of it. The Maitlands are in the hotel business and I'm afraid that they and Suzanne are bound to talk shop.'

Plans for Brocade. . . ? She said quickly, 'Thank you, no. I've got rather a lot to do, anyway.'

He looked at her, something which almost amounted to a question in his grey eyes, and she had a feeling that he wanted to say something but could not quite make up his mind. Then Johnny came up to them. Danny, Mark and Robin, rumpled and smoke-grimed but obviously blissfully happy, were clinging on to his arms.

He greeted Richard pleasantly, then pointed to the boys.

'I'm afraid they've got a bit black, Fran,' he said in laughing apology. 'I'll give you a hand to tub them, if you like.'

'Thanks, Johnny.' The boys loved being put to bed by Johnny, perhaps because he was always perfectly willing to turn bathtime into a mock-up of the Battle of Trafalgar!

'I see he believes in making himself useful,' Richard observed as Johnny went to say goodnight to Sam. 'A quite estimable young man.'

Fran looked at him, bewildered. There had been something suspiciously like a tinge of bitterness to that remark, but why? What had Johnny done to upset Richard? They had always seemed to get on quite well together.

She said quietly, 'Yes, he is,' but it seemed as though Richard had not even heard her. He had gone over to speak to Sam, who was leaning on his rake with the air of a man well satisfied with his work. The bonfire had burnt down to a pile of glowing ash, and Fran shivered suddenly, but not with cold. The conversation had left her with a queer sense of desolation, and she could not understand why.

Suzanne's and Richard's South African friends turned out to be a pleasant, middle-aged couple who were obviously entranced by the beauty of Brocade. Fran only caught a glimpse of them for they arrived just after she had put the children to bed and she was busy helping Mrs. Henderson in the kitchen. The previous evening Suzanne had given the housekeeper an elaborate menu and since many of the dishes required long and careful preparation she was glad of an extra pair of hands.

In actual fact, Fran thought, she looked far from

well. Her plump cheeks had lost their usual ruddy colour and her eyes looked heavy. She eventually admitted, in answer to Fran's anxious questioning, that her head ached and she felt cold and shivery. Very likely, she said, she was sickening for a summer cold.

She indignantly refused to allow Fran to wait at table, but as the evening progressed it became obvious that she was finding it increasingly difficult to keep going. It was with a sigh of relief that at last she sank into a chair and looked ruefully round the kitchen, stacked high with dirty plates and saucepans. Even with Fran's help there hadn't been time between courses to do the washing up.

'My! How I'd like to be able to wave a magic wand over this lot!' she said wearily. 'I'd give anything just to go to bed!'

'That's just where you are going.' Fran spoke firmly. 'I'm going to do the washing up. Oh yes!' as the housekeeper demurred. 'It won't take me long.'

'What won't?' Johnny, who had been spending the evening with a friend in the village, walked into the kitchen in time to hear Fran's words. When the situation was explained to him he took one look at his mother's white face and promptly sided with Fran.

'You go to bed with an aspirin or two, Mum, otherwise you'll be fit for nothing in the morning,' he decreed. 'I'll help Fran with the washing up. Don't forget you've trained me well—I'm a nifty hand with a tea towel.'

The housekeeper was feeling too ill to argue. She went up to bed protesting only feebly, leaving Fran and Johnny to tackle the pots and pans.

'Good heavens! How many people came to dinner? Twenty?' Johnny asked, pulling a comical face of dismay.

'Only two extra. But there were umpteen courses, don't forget,' Fran said drily.

'Poor old Mum! It would happen the first time she's feeling groggy! Never mind, we'll soon get this out of the way for her,' Johnny said cheerfully. 'She'll come down in the morning to find her kitchen as clean as a new pin!'

In spite of his optimism, however, the job took a long time and both were heartily sick of it by the time they had finished. Johnny gave a last triumphant polish to a big copper-bottomed saucepan and hung it up with a sigh of relief.

'Thank goodness that's over!' He looked at Fran, his merry face serious for once. 'You're a brick, Fran, doing this. There was no need to: it's not your job. Mum would have struggled through it somehow, ill-though she feels.'

'Don't be silly, Johnny. I'm glad to help. Your mother's been very good to us.'

Johnny put his arms round her and bending his head, kissed her gently on the forehead.

'Bless you.' It was simply and sincerely said: Johnny was very fond of his mother.

'I'm sorry to interrupt you, but I'd like to speak to Mrs. Henderson, if she's available.'

Johnny, whose back was towards the door, spun round. Richard was standing there, his face bleak.

Fran gave a slight gasp. Richard was the last person she had expected to see tonight. Furious with herself for the confusion that covered her, she stammered, 'She isn't here. She's gone to bed.'

'As I should doubtless have realised,' Richard said coldly. 'I merely wished to congratulate her on the excellent meal she served us tonight.' He glanced pointedly at the clock. 'I hope her efforts didn't exhaust her?'

Sarcasm was the thing Fran most hated. Flushing angrily, she said, 'She isn't feeling well. I made her go to bed. Johnny and I have been doing the washing up.'

She could tell from the set of his mouth and the cold scrutiny of his eyes that he was angry. He said harshly, 'I thought I had made it quite clear to you that you are a guest at Brocade, not a kitchenmaid. There's no need for you to feel that you ought occasionally to earn your keep.' He glanced meaningly at Johnny. 'Even when the job offers certain compensations.'

He had gone before either Fran or Johnny could think of a reply.

'Good lord!' Johnny was staring blankly after him. 'What on earth's bitten him?'

'I don't know.' Fran's voice shook a little in spite of herself. Richard's harshness had wounded her deeply.

'Seems to me he's a damn sight too high-handed at times!' Johnny's face was flushed: he was mortified on Fran's account as well as on his own. 'What the hell did he mean by compensations?'

Oddly enough, it never occurred to either of them that because Johnny's back had been turned towards the door, the nature of the embrace he had given Fran had been misinterpreted.

'I haven't the slightest idea.' Fran shrugged helplessly. 'Anyway, it doesn't matter.'

She tried to speak lightly, but she knew it did matter. She couldn't bear to think that Richard's attitude had changed towards her so completely. It was inexplicable. When he had returned to Brocade after those few days' absence he had greeted her with affection ... even, she thought, with a touch of tenderness. What had she done that he should now retreat into a shell of cold reserve? Had it anything to do with Suzanne? If so, it was unlikely that she would ever know.

Richard left Brocade early the next day, taking his guests with him. After they had gone Suzanne, who always looked sulky and bored whenever Richard was not in her immediate vicinity, wandered out into the garden where Fran and the children were playing ball.

Monday was the first to notice her. Despite several rebuffs he had not yet learned that Suzanne disliked all animals and on this occasion his welcome was particularly exuberant. Only Robin, who was nearest, saw Suzanne raise her foot slightly and kick the small furry bundle away, but everyone heard Monday's surprised and indignant yelp. In actual fact his feelings were more hurt than his person, but Robin's face became suffused with angry colour.

'You *kicked* him!' he accused Suzanne. 'You're a horrid, cruel woman! Fran says only bullies are unkind to animals, and that's what you are, a rotten bully!'

It was so unusual for Robin to raise his voice or utter a protest that for a moment Fran was speechless. Suzanne, however, was furious.

'I didn't kick the dog!' she declared angrily. 'How dare you tell such stories? You're a nasty, untruthful little boy, and if you're not careful a horrid man will come along with the big black bag he keeps to pop naughty children like you into!'

Such a threat would have been greeted with scorn by Beanie or Danny or Mark, but Robin was made of different metal. Fran saw his face whiten and his lips tremble slightly and spoke sharply.

'There's no such thing as a horrid man with a big black bag, Robin. All the same, you were very rude to Miss Pleydell. Please tell her you're sorry.'

'I didn't tell a story.' Robin's eyes were full of tears. 'She *did* kick Monday. I saw her.'

'I heard him yelp.' Mark and Danny spoke together, their eyes fixed accusingly on Suzanne. Too late she realised that her hasty denial had placed her in a distinctly awkward position.

The only course open to her was bravado. She turned angrily to Fran, who spoke quietly to the children.

'Go on playing, please, children. I'll deal with this.' She laid her hand on Robin's shoulder. 'I know you didn't tell a story, Robin. I heard Monday yelp, too. But I've no doubt that it was an accident and you must tell Miss Pleydell you're sorry for your rudeness.'

'Sorry,' Robin mumbled, and ran off.

Fran looked at Suzanne, whose face was white and tense with anger.

'I don't like being called a liar!'

'Neither did Robin,' Fran said quietly. She looked Suzanne straight in the eye. 'And since Monday certainly didn't yelp for nothing, I'm afraid I'm inclined to believe Robin.'

Suzanne gasped. 'Why, you little...! How dare you speak to me like that? I—I shall tell Richard!'

'Do!' Fran retorted, her quick temper firing. The last thing she had wanted at this juncture was a row with Suzanne, but it had been impossible to stand by and let poor Robin be unjustly accused of untruthfulness!

Suzanne glared, then she shrugged her shoulders contemptuously and went off without another word. Despite her threat Fran thought that the matter had ended there, but she was wrong.

She excused herself from dinner on the legitimate plea that she had a headache, but later, when she was crossing the hall, Richard poked his head round the door of the library and called her in.

Her heart beating wildly, Fran obeyed his summons. When she went into the room he was standing in front of the window, gazing out at the lengthening shadows. He turned, and she was completely unprepared for his tired, drawn face and the weariness of his eyes.

He came straight to the point. 'Suzanne appears to be extremely upset. She tells me that you quarrelled violently with her this afternoon and called her a liar in front of all the children. Was it really necessary for you to lose your temper quite so thoroughly?'

Fran went white. 'I did not call her a liar, nor do I think I was rude. Robin was, and I made him apologise.'

'Why was Robin rude? He hadn't struck me as that sort of child.'

'Didn't Suzanne tell you exactly what happened?' Fran kept her voice level with an effort.

'She said that there were so many wild accusations flying around that she couldn't keep track of them all. Frankly, it seems to me likely that it was all rather a tempest in a teapot, but I'm sorry if you found it necessary to be rude or insulting.'

The colour surged back into Fran's cheeks. 'I've already told you that I was neither!'

'Well, you are rather apt to get carried away when you're in a temper.' Richard's face was as expressionless as his voice. 'I must say I'm a little disappointed, particularly as I had especially asked you to make a friend of Suzanne.'

'She has made that very difficult.' Fran felt the angry tears pricking the back of her eyes. Richard appeared to have accepted Suzanne's version of this afternoon's incident unquestioningly and pride forbade her to give him hers.

For a long moment he said nothing. Fran was standing close enough to have touched him, but she felt as though they were standing on the opposite sides of an abyss. Then suddenly, unexpectedly, he sighed.

'All right, Fran. Let's leave it there, shall we? As you're leaving on Friday I don't suppose you'll see much more of Suzanne, and God knows I don't want your last memories of Brocade—and of me—to be unpleasant ones. Let's part friends.' He smiled at her, a faintly whimsical smile which nearly broke her heart. 'I did my best to snap your head off last night, didn't I? I'm sorry about that. I was—tired, though that's no excuse. I'm glad you were kind enough to help Mrs. Henderson: I've noticed she has a bad cold.'

Bewildered by his sudden change of front, Fran stood there dumbly. Richard glanced at his watch and said gently, 'I think that's all. I've a telephone call to make. Goodnight, my dear. Be happy.'

'Be happy' ... Why did he say that? what did he mean? Her thoughts tumultuous, she walked quickly out of the room, not daring to stay lest she lose control, but at the door she turned for a last look. Richard, his arms folded across his chest, was staring up at the portrait of his uncle which hung above the mantelpiece and the likeness between them, suddenly sharply accentuated, was not pleasant to see.

CHAPTER TWELVE

As September ran out in dry, sunny weather so the atmosphere at Brocade seemed to Fran to grow more strained. She found herself almost glad that in a few days' time she and the children would be returning to London, for the tension was beginning to tell on her nerves. She hardly ever saw Richard, Suzanne was openly hostile, and even Mrs. Henderson, struggling with a heavy cold, seemed burdened and unlike her usual cheerful self.

The housekeeper was less worried about Johnny than she had been, since she was gradually becoming convinced that his Eiluned would be a steadying influence in his life, rather than the reverse, but her future plans seemed uncertain. To be sure, Richard had promised her that she could continue to work at Brocade, but he did not say in what capacity and something in his attitude had discouraged questions.

She was sad, too, at the prospect of losing Fran and the children. During their stay at Brocade she had become genuinely fond of them all and felt that without them the old house would seem very lonely and empty. (Not, possibly, that she'd have much chance to miss them. If the place was going to be overrun by workmen she would have her hands full tidying up after them, she thought grimly.)

Rosemary, too, felt a pang of regret when she heard that a definite date had been fixed for the exodus from Brocade. She had been drawn to Fran from the moment they had first met and wished now that she had done a little more to further a friendship which she knew Michael had desired for her but which had seemed to be fraught with so many complications.

Much as she had liked Fran she had also envied her: she always seemed so gay and full of life and so happy with her 'adopted' family. Not, Rosemary had to admit to herself, that that was really surprising, because they were nice children. No wonder Michael was so interested in them! He would have liked to have seen a lot more of them: it was entirely her fault, she thought remorsefully, that he hadn't.

For a long time she wrestled with her conscience, then she picked up the receiver and dialled Brocade's number. Would Fran like to bring the children to tea before they returned to London?

'I ought to have asked you a long time ago,' she added with rueful honesty, 'but I just didn't get around to it. I kept telling myself that there was plenty of time. I hope that it isn't too late now?'

She so obviously meant what she said that Fran accepted the invitation gladly. It would cheer the children up. They were all very subdued at the thought of leaving Brocade, especially as it would also mean saying goodbye to Monday. Her one consolation was that she knew that with the marvellous resilience of children they would soon adapt themselves to their old home again and settle down perfectly happily. If only she, too, could be sure of the same resilience... !

On the day of Rosemary's tea party there was an unexpected letter from Miss Challoner. Danny's and Beanie's mother had died in hospital without ever recovering consciousness.

Fran's eyes blurred as she read the words. She dreaded the thought of breaking the news to the two children, even though they had become so used to their mother's absence that probably it would not be the shock it once would have been. There would be tears, of course, but they were too young to realise that now a big question mark hung over their whole future.

Because that was Fran's way, she forgot her own

emotional problems in her concern for the two orphans. In fact, she was glad to put an end to the weary circling of her thoughts. She could not give way to despair while the children needed her: for the second time they would be her buttress against the blows that life dealt her.

She decided against telling Beanie and Danny about their mother straightaway, since she did not want to cloud what would otherwise be a joyous occasion. However, though she made a great effort she could not quite disguise her own sadness and Rosemary was quick to sense that something was wrong.

In the kitchen, where Fran was helping her with the preparations for tea, she turned to her with a blunt question.

'Is anything the matter, Fran? Can I help?'

Fran hesitated, but the children were out in the garden with Michael and the longing to confide in a sympathetic friend proved too much.

'I've had bad news about Danny's and Beanie's mother. She died in hospital yesterday: I haven't told them yet.'

'I'm very sorry.' Rosemary's face was grave, for she knew the children's story. Instinctively she looked out of the window. All five children were romping on the lawn with Michael: he was sitting down with Danny on his shoulders and the others scrambling all over him. She realised with a stab of pain that it was a long time since she'd seen her husband look so happy. (He'd been thrilled when he'd heard about her invitation ... had taken special pains to ensure that he'd have a free afternoon.)

'What will happen to Danny and Beanie now?' she asked sombrely.

'That's what's worrying me. There aren't any relatives willing to take them. I suppose that under certain circumstances adoption might be the answer, but...' She left the sentence unfinished.

Rosemary was still looking out of the window, her eyes on the laughing children. For a moment she was silent, then she said, almost reluctantly, 'They're nice kids, aren't they?'

'Yes. But very unfortunate.' Fran's voice was bitter. 'Just a few short months ago they had everything that children could possibly wish for—a nice home, devoted parents. Then some criminal lunatic careers along on the wrong side of the road, smashes into the family car, and everything's over. Just like that.'

'But they love you, and you make them happy,' Rosemary protested.

'It isn't the same.' Unconsciously Fran repeated the very same words that Mrs. Henderson had once used.

And they may not always have you, Rosemary thought. A question was trembling on her lips, but she dared not ask it. Somehow she did n.. think that the change in Fran was entirely due to her anxiety over Danny and Beanie. She looked very pale and her shadowed eyes suggested that she had not been sleeping well. She was nothing like the sparkling, radiant girl who had come to dinner with Richard Quayle such a short while ago.

Richard Quayle! Rosemary gave a strawberry jelly an energetic shake to loosen it from the sides of the mould and rather wished that it was Richard she was shaking instead. She and Michael had both suspected, the night he and Fran had come to dinner, that the friendship between the two was developing into something deeper. But that, of course, had been before Suzanne Pleydell had arrived on the scene.

Rosemary frowned to herself. Suzanne had been charming on the one occasion they had met, but she had not liked her. She was a fairly good judge of character and the hint of hardness about Suzanne's mouth and eyes had not escaped her notice. She wasn't a patch on Fran, but nevertheless it looked very much as though Richard had passed the gold up for the glitter. And it also looked as though he had made poor Fran wretched in the process. She was the sort of girl who would care deeply if she cared at all.

Robin came running in to ask for a drink of water at that moment and so nothing more was said. Fran noticed, however, that although Rosemary did everything she could to make all the children feel happy and at home, there was a special gentleness in her dealings with Beanie and Danny which could only be explained by a deep compassion. She and Michael would have made wonderful parents, she thought regretfully, and this would have been an ideal home for any child. The atmosphere was just right ... safe and friendly and warm. They all felt it.

In Michael's car, going home, Beanie nestled up to her and she could feel the glowing warmth of her small body through the thin stuff of her cotton dress. Her usually pale face was rosy with contentment.

'We've had a lovely time, haven't we?' she said drowsily. She liked Mrs. Coates nearly as much as she liked Fran. She'd got a 'Mummy-face'. (Beanie could not have said exactly what she meant by that, but she knew it was something to do with a person's eyes and the way she smiled. Miss Pleydell hadn't got a 'Mummy-face' at all, but perhaps Mr. Quayle didn't mind about that.)

She wasn't a fusser, either. Beanie hated fussers. She didn't seem to mind in the least when Danny started with the chocolate biscuits and the sponge fingers and finished with the egg sandwiches. She agreed that it was more usual the other way round, but if Danny was happy why worry? And she didn't look a bit cross when Robin spilt his tea all over the pretty embroidered tablecloth, just said it would wash out. And she'd given her, Beanie, a big apron and let her help with the washing-up and never once told her she'd have to be careful. (She had been, of course: the china was so pretty, with little pink rosebuds all over it.)

Fran looked down at the small sleepy figure and her arm tightened round her. It seemed cruel to spoil what had been such a happy day, but it couldn't be helped. Tonight she and Danny would have to be told about their mother: the evil moment couldn't be put off any longer.

In the end it was not as painful as Fran had feared. The children took the news bravely: perhaps, she thought, because they were a little too young to understand the full extent of their loss. Nonetheless, there was a quiver in Beanie's voice as she asked, 'What will happen to us now, Fran?' and later, when Fran went to tuck her up, she saw tearstains on her cheeks.

'Better take them out somewhere nice tomorrow so they don't brood over things,' Mrs. Henderson counselled. 'What about a trip to Cheltenham? Johnny's got to go and I know he'd be glad to take you.'

This seemed a good idea, for the children had already said that they wanted to buy Mrs. Henderson and Sam a goodbye present. There ought to be one for Richard, too, but she didn't know what they could give him. Anything they chose would be so hopelessly inadequate. She supposed, too, that she would have to thank him for all the weeks they had enjoyed his hospitality, and the thought filled her with dread. She only hoped Suzanne would be there as well. There would be less fear of spilling her emotions all over him if Suzanne was an amused, bored and slightly contemptuous onlooker.

'Milady's gone to London to get her hair done,' Mrs. Henderson informed her at breakfast the next morning. 'She and Mr. Richard are going to a big ball at a posh London hotel tonight, did you know? He took her to the station, but he's come back again. Seems he's got an important appointment this afternoon and he won't be driving up to London until later this evening.'

Fran said nothing. She had heard Suzanne discussing that ball with Richard. She had had the distinct impression that Richard was not at all keen, but evidently Suzanne had managed to get her own way. She had a sudden vision of Suzanne's lovely, pliant figure in Richard's arms ... her cheek against his ... and set her teeth. There was no need to torment herself unnecessarily.

'Fran, Sue isn't eating any breakfast.'

Beanie's gentle little voice recalled her thoughts. Sue was indeed not eating: she had pushed her plate away and her bottom lip was trembling.

'Don't want anything to eat. I've got a *dretful* pain in my middle!' she sobbed, clutching her small tummy with both hands.

'Oh, darling! I *am* sorry!' Fran lifted her gently off the chair, her face anxious. She always hated it when the children were not well.

'I feel sick!' Sue moaned.

She was very sick. Fran hoped that afterwards she might feel better, but she continued to complain of a tummyache and was so fretful and unlike herself that Fran was forced to tell Johnny that the Cheltenham trip was off.

'Colly-wobbles,' said Mrs. Henderson knowingly. 'Did she eat any green apples yesterday?'

Fran shook her head. 'She hasn't been out of my sight.'

Sue was sick again, and when Fran took her temperature she found that it was slightly up. She stood looking down at the child, her brow creased into a troubled frown. Somehow or another this seemed to be something more than the usual tummy 'upset'.

'I don't like it. I think I'll ring Dr. Coates just to be on the safe side,' she told Mrs. Henderson. She went to the telephone and dialled Michael's number, but it was Rosemary who answered.

'Oh ... Rosemary! Fran here. Is Michael in, please? Sue's got rather a bad tummyache and I'm a bit bothered about her.'

'He isn't in just at the moment, Fran. He went out to a confinement at about eight o'clock this morning and isn't back yet. I shouldn't think he'll be long, though.'

'There's no way I can reach him?'

' 'Fraid not. Those people live in a rather out-of-the-way place and they're not on the phone. Is it really urgent, Fran?'

Fran hesitated. 'Well ... no, not urgent. But I'd like Michael to look at her as soon as he comes back.' She knew that Michael would understand her anxiety. He wouldn't call her over-anxious or over-fussy.

'Of course. I'll tell him the moment he comes in. Poor Sue! I hope it wasn't something she had here that hasn't agreed with her,' Rosemary said.

Fran put down the receiver and went back to Sue. The tummyache didn't seem to be any better and she only seemed comforted when Fran was holding her. The other children, looking concerned, at first tried to think of things to amuse her, but soon realised that she wanted to be left alone.

By lunchtime, the fear of appendicitis uppermost in her mind, Fran was almost beside herself with worry. In desperation she rang Rosemary again.

'He hasn't come home yet, Fran.' Rosemary, too, sounded anxious. 'Look, if you're really worried shall I give you the telephone numbers of one or two other doctors in the area?'

Fran hesitated. 'I'd rather have Michael, of course, and so would Sue, I know. But ... yes, please, Rosemary, I think I ought to do something.'

Rosemary gave her three telephone numbers and Fran began a round of calls. Ten minutes later she put the receiver down with a shrug of despair. One doctor was off-duty and she was told by a machine, playing a recorded message, to ring Michael's number. Both of the other two doctors were out on cases. There was no help for it, she thought, she would have to wait for Michael willy-nilly.

She told Rosemary what had happened and then went to sit by Sue and wait for Michael to make an appearance. The child was now so pale that there was an almost transparent look about her and Fran felt herself go cold. Sue had never been strong. Supposing... ?

It was not until late afternoon that Michael's car swept to a stop outside the house.

'Hello, Fran!' Michael greeted her with his usual breezy cheerfulness. 'Rosemary says you're bothered about young Sue. Sorry to have been so long answering your call, but I've been tied up with a long and difficult confinement. What appears to be the trouble?'

Fran told him, and his cheerfulness vanished almost immediately he saw Sue's pale, pinched little face. He made a swift but thorough examination and then his diagnosis confirmed Fran's worst fears.

'Appendicitis,' he said tersely. 'Acute, too. I'll ring for an ambulance. She'll have to be operated on immediately.'

Afterwards Fran could never clearly recall the next few hours. The ride to the hospital in the ambulance with Sue, wrapped in blankets, held in her arms ... the kindness of the nurse who admitted them ... the grave face of the tall, fair-haired young man who examined Sue ... the last glimpse of the child as she was whisked away to be prepared for the operation ... all formed a mass of jumbled, kaleidoscopic impressions which whirled madly around in her head. Eventually she found herself waiting, alone, in a tiny room: she could not bear to leave the hospital while the operation was still in progress and she knew that Mrs. Henderson would look after the other children. She clenched her hands convulsively, fear such as she had never known before taking hold of her. She tried desperately to keep herself from disintegrating, but the loneliness of her vigil was almost more than she could bear. How long would the operation take? How long would she have to endure this dreadful waiting?

The door opened and she looked up fearfully, expecting to see a doctor or nurse. Instead, her eyes widened in stunned disbelief as she saw Richard ... Richard, hard-faced, and his eyes full of a desperate anxiety.

'Fran!' He crossed the room in two quick strides and sat down beside her, covering her icy hands with his own strong, warm ones. 'My dear, I came as soon as I got back and heard from Mrs. Henderson what had happened. How is Sue?'

There was no time to question or wonder at his presence. Conscious of new strength and hope pouring into her at Richard's touch, she said unsteadily 'They're operating now. It's hard ... waiting ...'

'I know. I thought you'd need someone.' Richard's voice was quiet. He began chafing her hands with his own. 'My dear, you're absolutely frozen! Would you like me to see if I can get you a hot drink?'

Fran shook her head. 'No. Please don't leave me.' It did not even occur to her, in this time of crisis, to dissemble. Her defences were bare.

He said nothing, but the clasp of his hands tightened. They sat without moving or speaking, and his warmth sent a glow through her cold, tired body. All her thoughts were centred on Sue, but it was Richard who supplied her with courage and with hope. For how long they sat there she never afterwards knew, but it seemed an eternity before the door of the waiting room again opened. It was the tall, fair-haired young man. He looked desperately tired, but he was smiling, and at the sight of his smile Fran's whole face lit up.

'The operation has been a complete success. She's come through it remarkably well.'

The magic words were still sounding in Fran's ears when a little later, and still in silence, she and Richard walked to his car, which was parked in a corner of the hospital forecourt. Richard held the door open for her and got in beside her, but he did not switch on the engine. It was very quiet, and the moon had momentarily hidden her face behind a mass of cloud. Fran did not know she was crying until she tasted the salt on her lips, nor did the man realise it until a shaft of moonlight lit up her face and showed him the smudge of tears on her pale cheeks. He lifted his hand and laid it gently across her eyes, feeling the long, wet lashes tremble like butterfly wings under his touch.

'Oh, Fran! Darling, don't cry!' He put his arms round her, holding her with tender strength, pressing her head against him while she cried unrestrainedly.

'Finished?' he asked gently when after a few moments the sobs ceased.

'Yes,' said Fran, gulping. For a moment she rested against him in that close protective clasp, feeling a sense of utter peace and security, then, remembering, she drew herself quickly away and blew her nose defiantly.

'I'm sorry. I didn't mean to weep all over you.'

He ignored that. 'Fran,' he said gently, 'there's something I'd like you to know. When I discovered that you were here alone I tried to find Johnny for you. If he had been available I wouldn't have come. Believe me, I knew that I'd be a poor substitute. But if it helped just a little to have a friend with you ... well then, I'm more than glad.'

'Johnny?' Fran's voice was sharp with incredulity. 'I don't understand. Why should you think I wanted Johnny?'

There was a moment's silence. Then Richard said,

in an odd, strained sort of voice 'I thought that he and you ... you were always together...'

Fran drew a long breath. 'You didn't think— Richard, you *couldn't* have thought there was anything between Johnny and me? Why? Oh, I'm fond of him, of course, he's an absolute dear. But as for anything else...' She shook her head helplessly.

There was another long silence. Then, very carefully, Richard said, 'You mean ... you're not in love with him?'

'Certainly not!' Fran spoke indignantly. 'He—why, he's almost like one of the children!'

She looked so ruffled that in spite of himself Richard had to laugh. 'A rather precocious child!' He paused, looking not at her but out into the darkness. Then he said slowly, 'I seem to have been a little— dense. You see, that's what I thought—that Johnny was rather like one of the family—until Suzanne ... until someone ... said something that seemed to indicate a big romance was brewing. I used my eyes after that and I couldn't help noticing that you and he were on the best possible terms. Even then I might have trusted to my own instincts if I hadn't heard Mrs. Henderson tell one of the daily helps that she thought Johnny was far too young to get married but she had the consolation of knowing that he'd fallen in love with a wonderful girl. Whom did she mean, if she didn't mean you?'

'Johnny's going to marry an Irish girl named Eiluned. He talks about her non-stop, day and night,' Fran told him, a laugh shaking her voice. She stopped, suddenly shy. 'Whatever you imagined about us, Richard, you were way off beam. There's no room for anyone but Eiluned in Johnny's affections, I can assure you of that!'

'Good God!' said Richard slowly. 'What a fool I've been!' He looked at her then, his grey eyes suddenly intent, and, absurdly, her heart began to race. 'So when you were holding my hand ... in there ... I wasn't just a substitute for Johnny?'

Fran felt the tell-tale colour creep up under her skin but she answered him steadily.

'No, Richard. You weren't a substitute.'

He drew a short breath. 'You mean...?' He stopped. Then suddenly and incredibly his arms were around her again: his mouth found hers and she was held, fiercely, in his embrace. She could feel the wild beating of his heart pressed so tightly against her body and felt the blood racing madly through her own veins.

It was a long time later that she said, 'Richard ... what about Suzanne?'

'Suzanne?' Richard repeated the name abstractedly, as though it meant nothing to him. Then he stared at her in sudden, rueful dismay and clapped his hand to his head. 'Dear heaven! Fran, I've forgotten her very existence for the last few hours! And I was supposed to take her to a ball tonight! I was just going to get ready when Mrs. Henderson buttonholed me and told me all about Sue. After that, I forgot about everyone and everything except you.'

There was a long silence, each thinking of Suzanne's mounting fury as the minutes ticked relentlessly away and there was no sign of Richard. She would never forgive a slight like that.

Fran said hesitantly, 'If you don't want to tell me, Richard, it doesn't matter. But ... I couldn't help thinking that perhaps she was someone special.'

He answered her gravely. 'She was never special, Fran. I first met her through her father, who was a great friend of my stepfather's. I liked her ... I won't say I didn't. She is very beautiful and at one time I found her excellent company. We had a good time together ... all on the surface, you understand, nothing deeper.'

He paused to kiss her again, very gentle kisses on

her closed eyelids.

'I never thought she was interested in marriage, least of all to me. Then Brocade was more or less dumped in my lap and, as I've told you, I didn't know what the devil to do with it. Like a fool I mentioned my predicament to Suzanne and she immediately tried to sell me the idea of turning it into a hotel. She was so mad keen to do it that I suppose she more or less infected me with her enthusiasm. Certainly I thought she was looking at the whole thing from a business angle, though I realise now that she probably thought it would give her some sort of hold over me.'

Fran said soberly, 'I hope she won't feel let down.' (Some day she must tell Richard about Bryan ... he had the right to know.)

'She has no right to feel that,' Richard reassured her quickly. 'Believe me, Fran, I made it absolutely plain to her right from the very beginning that I wasn't the slightest bit in love with her and if she had any thought that I might some day marry her I can assure you that she was merely deluding herself.' He paused. 'I also made it quite clear to her, before she came to England, that I hadn't really made up my mind about Brocade. I told her I wanted time to think things over, but she wasn't prepared to wait.'

Fran looked at him, her eyes bright. 'How long have you known, Richard? That you didn't want Brocade to be turned into a hotel, I mean, and—and about me?'

She saw the smile that she loved light up his dark face. 'I knew for sure I didn't want Brocade to be turned into a hotel the night I drove you home after we'd had dinner with Rosemary and Michael. I'd had several misgivings already and your remarks served to crystallise my doubts. The trouble was, I didn't know what to do about Suzanne. She is so self-willed and obstinate that I knew she'd do her damnedest to make me fall in with her plans. In the end I'm afraid I rather hoped that if I dithered long enough she'd lose interest without it coming to a rather unpleasant show-down.

'As for you, my darling'—he picked up her hand and held it against his cheek—'I knew that I was in love with you the day I came home and found you arranging the flowers. I'd been attracted to you from the start——'

'Even when I called you names?' Fran asked provocatively, stroking his lean brown cheek.

'Even then. I fought against it, of course. I didn't want a wife. Like Uncle Antony, I had no use for emotional ties. But you, heart's dearest, you wore down my defences ... and then when I found I was in love with you I thought it was too late. I was almost crazy with jealousy of Johnny, until I saw the look on your face, the night I rowed you in the library, and I realised what a selfish brute I was. I made up my mind after that that all that mattered was your happiness and I wouldn't spoil it.'

Fran laughed shakily. 'I couldn't understand why you'd changed so much.'

He looked at her. 'It's the first time in my life I've ever tried to put someone else's happiness before my own. You did that for me, Fran. I was even going to let Suzanne have her own way about Brocade ... with you gone, I knew I couldn't bear to live in it. It is you and the children who have turned it into a home. Before that, even in Uncle Antony's day, it was just a beautiful, empty shell.'

'Will you stay in England now? Or go back to Johannesburg?'

'Do you mind?'

'No,' Fran said simply. 'As long as I'm with you I don't care where I live.'

After that, it was impossible to speak for a very long time. When at last Richard raised his head he said huskily, 'You don't want a long engagement, do you?

Can we get married right away?'

Her face showed her dismay. 'Oh ... Richard! I'd love to, of course, but I can't leave the children in the lurch. They must get used gradually to the idea of being without me ... get to know the person who'll take my place.'

He laughed a little ruefully. 'I've always had to share you with those wretched children! Oh, don't worry, my love!' as she shot him a swift, anxious look. 'I don't really mean it. I want the children to be happy, too.' He glanced at his watch. 'My sweet, it's very, very late. I've no doubt you intend to return to the hospital first thing tomorrow morning, so you must try and snatch a few hours' sleep first.'

Fran's face set in anxious lines. 'I do want to be with Sue as much as possible, the first few days at least. The hospital want that, too: they don't believe in children being separated from their parents at a time like this, and I'm a mother-substitute for Sue, if nothing else. But I'm worried about the others. Mrs. Henderson is a dear, but she's got her hands full already.'

Richard laughed. 'You needn't worry your head about that. Directly you and Sue had left for the hospital, apparently, Rosemary came over and took all the children back to her house. She told Mrs. Henderson she'd look after them until Sue was better.'

Fran was speechless with surprise. Rosemary to the rescue again. Perhaps, though, she ought not to be surprised. She had proved before that she was a friend in need ... in times of crisis her generosity was great enough to overcome her bitterness.

Suzanne was so furious about Richard's failure to turn up at the ball that she did not even bother to read the letter of explanation and apology that he wrote to her. She had telephoned Brocade while he was at the hospital, and on hearing from Mrs. Henderson where he had gone and why she had realised once and for all that she had gambled ... and lost. At her request her belongings were sent on to her and when Fran saw the suitcases being taken out of the front door she knew, with a sense of relief, that Suzanne had passed out of their lives for ever.

The news of her engagement was greeted with delight by everyone ... her parents, Miss Challoner, Mrs. Henderson, Johnny ('Don't you dare beat me to the altar!' he threatened), Rosemary and Michael. The last to be told were the children. They spent a blissful time with Rosemary and Michael while Sue was in hospital, but on the day she was discharged they were all gathered on the lawn at Brocade to give her a tumultuous welcome.

It was after the excitement had died down a little that Beanie's sharp eyes noticed a new state of affairs.

'Fran!' she exclaimed wonderingly. 'You're holding Mr. Quayle's hand!'

'Yes. We're going to be married,' Fran told her, and held her breath. Even in the midst of her radiant happiness she could not help wondering how the children would react to this news.

Beanie regarded her gravely. Then, 'You're not wearing a ring,' she pointed out disapprovingly.

Richard turned to Fran, a laugh in his grey eyes. He took the signet ring off his little finger and slipped it on to the third finger of her left hand.

'It's a bit big, my darling, but will it do until we can get you a proper one?'

Fran laughed and nodded, and Beanie nodded too, her sense of propriety satisfied.

'Now you're *properly* going to get married,' she asserted. She wrinkled her brow, something else she'd been told about engagements and weddings coming into her mind. 'Can I be a bridesmaid?'

Richard looked at Fran. 'Certainly,' she said promptly.

'And Sue?'

'Of course.'

'Can we wear long dresses and have flowers in our hair?'

'You may,' Fran said, and then, as Beanie sighed in satisfaction, Rosemary said mischievously, 'And the boys can be pageboys, can't they, Fran? Won't they look sweet in blue velvet trousers and frilly white shirts?'

They looked at her in horror, aghast to find her such a traitor.

'No, thank you,' said Mark firmly.

''Spect we'll be back in London by then,' said Robin.

'We'll look after Monday. You don't want him messing up your wedding,' Danny suggested.

Rosemary looked after their retreating figures and laughed. Bright-eyed and serene, the lines of bitterness had disappeared miraculously from her pretty face. A large part of her unhappiness had been caused by her intense frustration, which had choked her natural lovingness. Now Mark and Danny and Robin had set her free and her reactions were normal again. The last week had shown her the folly of living with her sterile bitterness and the joy that could come through the warm and loving hearts of children who needed her as much as she needed them.

She said, a little shyly, 'Fran, I've got something to tell you. Your Miss Challoner came to see us the other day, to make sure the children were all right. Michael and I told her that if it's possible, some time later on, we'd like to adopt Danny and Beanie. We—we love them already and I think—well, I think they quite like us.'

'Rosemary!' Fran's face was radiant. 'Oh, that's the most wonderful wedding present I could possibly be given!'

No one, she thought humbly, had the right to feel

so joyful. To have Richard ... and Brocade ... and Rosemary and Michael as friends and neighbours ... and Danny and Beanie growing up before her eyes, both giving and receiving happiness....

'We'd like them all,' Rosemary said soberly. 'It isn't possible, of course, but I hope we'll be able to have the others for holidays sometimes. You've made them into a real family, Fran, and I don't think they'll ever forget that family feeling.'

Fran's eyes were shining. They shone again, two days later, when Richard gave her what Beanie would have called a 'proper' engagement ring. He put it on her finger in the library at Brocade, where the westering sun was turning everything into patterns of gold.

'Oh!' she exclaimed, catching her breath. 'It's beautiful!' She held up her small brown hand so that the ring sparkled red and white fire in the sunlight. 'My hands aren't elegant enough to show it off!' she added ruefully.

'Don't be ashamed of them. They're the gentlest hands I know,' Richard told her, and carried the small, work-roughened palm to his lips. Fran looked up at Sir Antony's portrait, her eyes suddenly thoughtful.

'I'm sure he must disapprove intensely!' she said with a slight laugh.

This time Richard kissed her lips. 'Don't you believe it. If Uncle Antony had ever been lucky enough to meet a girl like you he'd never have led such a lonely and miserable life.' He traced her eyebrows with the tips of his fingers. 'Have I ever told you that I love the way your eyebrows go up at the tips ... like swallows' wings?'

She said dreamily, 'To think I'll be here when the swallows come next spring ... Richard, are you really sure that you want to live here and not in South Africa? Much as I love Brocade, I couldn't be happy here unless you were happy too.'

'That relieves my mind. I've sometimes been afraid that you're only marrying me because you like my house so much,' he said, laughing at her indignant face. He touched her shining hair lightly. 'Not that it will be my house much longer. I shall give it to you for a wedding present ... with one stipulation.'

'And that is?'

'That you're never to more than half fill it with children "in care".' He laughed again at the startled question in her eyes.

'We'll need the other half for all our little Quayles, won't we?' he said, and took her hand in his. Then, together, they walked out of the open french windows into the warm and golden air and went in search of Beanie to show her the diamond and ruby ring.

Each month from Harlequin

8 NEW FULL LENGTH ROMANCE NOVELS

Listed below are the last three months' releases:

These titles are available at your local bookseller, or through the Harlequin Reader Service, M.P.O. Box 707, Niagara Falls, N.Y. 14302; Canadian address 649 Ontario St., Stratford, Ont. N5A 6W4.

Have You Missed Any of These
Harlequin Romances?

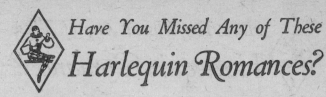